G l

O f

H o p e

François Sigrist

Averette Publications, Inc.
USA

GLIMMER OF HOPE

©1998 by François Sigrist and A. D. Miller, Editor

First Edition: January 1998
Printed in the United States of America

ISBN 0-966-03400-7

DEDICATED
TO THE PEOPLE OF THE
UNITED STATES OF AMERICA
WHO HAVE WELCOMED ME TO THEIR
COUNTRY WITH WARMTH AND GENEROSITY.
IN APPRECIATION
A PERCENTAGE FROM THE SALE OF
THIS NOVEL WILL BE DONATED TO CHARITIES
WORKING TO IMPROVE THE PLIGHT OF THE
HOMELESS, ABUSED, AND ILLITERATE.

Prologue

Tearing the t-shirt off my back, my instinct was to continue to actually rip the skin off my bones — it felt too tight, and the panic was making my heart visibly leap out of my chest. My breathing was painfully difficult. I was frozen and could barely stand on my rubbery legs — my knees buckling from running. My mind swirled, *What is this place? Where am I? How long had I been wandering in the maze of the city?*

My legs had carried me into a surreal part of the city that was totally unfamiliar to me. Not knowing how long I had been running made it impossible to know how I had ended up in this questionable neighborhood.

It was pointless trying to figure out the answers to the endless string of questions running through my mind. Mind — what mind? With my memory diminishing daily, how could I put my thoughts in any kind of order? I felt fortunate if I remembered my own name in the web of mishaps thrown at me by the universe. *How could someone play with my life without my consent or knowledge?* The insanity of the thought defied explanation

The streets were dark as far as I could see. The only cars were permanently parked with parts missing. I broke the silence only by my footsteps as I crushed the glass or paper under my shoe.

A siren in the distance. No one to notice my appearance — sweat pouring from my face, dirt glued to my skin, t-shirt hanging from my waist, hair tangled and matted, a dazed look in my eyes. I could barely shuffle my feet with legs weakened from running.

Heaps of smelling garbage littered the street. As I passed an open door, the reeking smell of alcohol and stale smoke nauseated me. When three men staggered out of the door, I had to fight to keep from losing my balance and steadied myself against the damp, slippery wall. Instinctively I knew that I had to find a lighted, crowded street for safety.

As I pushed myself away from the wall, my legs finally gave out and folded beneath me. My body lurched forward with my knees hitting the asphalt followed by my face crashing to the ground. Lying in the street with gravel deeply embedded in my face and both knees bleeding from the fall, I felt one eye start to swell. The burning sensation of the open wounds made me realize that I had no more strength to run. It crossed my mind that I could die here in the street with no one to hear my plea for help.

Crawling over to the curb I could hear my life force leaving with a whistling from my lungs. I shut my eyes and thought that maybe this was the end. I was exhausted and couldn't even imagine getting to my feet.

I came to with the feeling that someone was standing over me. Opening my eyes I couldn't see anything, but heard "Get up, Alex. I'll help you." I felt the silent force getting stronger, pouring vitality into me, propelling me forward, picking up speed, defying the reality of my exhausted body, and pushing my lungs to the brink of exploding.

There were lights in the distance. I could see cars. The lights and noises were real. I was back to civilization. The pain was entirely too real now that I had involuntarily slowed down, but I felt safe for the moment.

I'm a bloody mess, I thought as I stepped back into the shadow of the building. Across the street in an open mall I saw a drop box for donated articles. *Just what I need.* I crossed the street limping from the pain in my knees. Going through a couple of boxes, I found my new wardrobe — a clean t-shirt and a baseball cap. Wiping the blood and gravel from my face with the remains of my torn shirt, I slipped on the clean shirt and placed the cap on my head, and I felt like a new man.

The heat from the steam off the coffee brought me back to reality with no idea of how I ended up here or how much time had gone by. I glanced around the small restaurant filled with the smell of fresh, crisp french fries. The waitress taking an order a few tables down exchanged kind words with two truck drivers looking for a short route to the interstate. A full cup of black steaming coffee sat in front of me with a glass of ice water on my left. Slowly I crumpled my paper napkin and dabbed it into the water and with gentle strokes, I bathed my lacerated face, carefully removed the remaining gravel. Grabbing a piece of ice, I placed it on my swollen eye before rubbing the remaining ice on my stiff neck.

I must remain calm and try to remember back to when all of this started, was my first thought as I continued to sit with the hot coffee in front of me. After three or four more sips I relaxed a little and acknowledged that I was actually feeling better.

Looking around I quickly assessed the situation still wondering where I was. None of the customers looked threatening, and the waitress seemed awfully pleasant. Had it not been for the stinging of my scraped face and hands, I might have thought all this was a dream — no, a nightmare — that I wouldn't wish on my worst enemy.

"Can I freshen up your coffee?" A smiling face wearing a t-shirt with a Florida Everglade logo was standing right in front of me holding a pot of steaming brew.

That's a place I'd rather be right now, I thought to myself, but answered returning her smile with, "Why not? The coffee's great."

"Let me know if you need anything else. My name is Sharon," she offered as she poured another cup.

"Hi, Sharon. I'm Alex. Thank you for your kindness, and do you have the time?"

"Four AM," she replied as she moved away.

Four in the morning. Another reality check. I must have been totally out of my head, running all night with no recollection. I needed to get home, soak in a hot bath and then try to make sense of the last twenty-four hours.

As I extracted myself from the booth, leaving a buck and some change on the table I waived at Sharon and walked outside. *What a relief*, I thought to myself when I realized that I recognized the area. Jack and I had dropped off a car not too far from here and had actually stopped for coffee and a donut at this same place. Talk about selective memory. *Why would I remember this dump?* Just another question without an answer. Oh, well, the streets were deserted and quiet, and I could find my way home from here.

In less than an hour I arrived at my apartment, climbed the three flights of stairs with difficulty, opened the front door and staggered inside. Closing the door behind me, I leaned against it and breathed a huge sigh of relief.

Rick was sitting on the sofa talking to One Eye. I saw them talking, but their words didn't cut through my haze. Can't stop now, as I used the absolute last of my energy to make it to the bathroom, turned on the hot water, dropped my clothes in a pile in the middle of the floor where I stood, and eased myself slowly into the healing liquid. I felt the warmth seeping into my tired and battered body. I was safe at last.

What has happened to me?

F r a n ç o i s   S i g r i s t

Part One

$\mathbf{T}$he few remaining fragments of my memory made it a difficult task to remember the details of my childhood. Only the highlights of my youth remained, and those were somewhat vague. There was no rhyme or reason, no emotions attached to my memories, and worst of all no reliability of their presence from one day to another.

I was born nineteen years prior to the incident I just related, just five minutes after my twin brother Adam. From that day forward nothing could separate us. Our mother died after delivering us. "Complications," was all that the doctors had told my dad. He, of course, took her death very hard, and even after we were old enough to understand what complications were, Dad still could not talk about her. So I never really knew what happened.

With twins to take care of, he had turned over the day-to-day operation of his business to his partner. We never experienced a mother, so we never felt deprived. Plus, we had each other.

My father believed in positive thinking, and to me it seemed as if everything came easily to him. He seldom got upset, and if he did, he stayed calm, never raised his voice and made everything a learning experience. Patiently he would take the time to explain, and I do remember early in my life seeing him as a source of strength and security. His wonderful sense of humor and his habit of playing practical jokes were kind of his trademarks.

One memory that stuck in my mind was a warm spring day

when he jumped in his car and rolled down the window as he was backing out of the driveway and said, "Okay, you two, behave. I'll be back in a couple of hours." He waved as the car pulled away.

Sure enough, after three and a half hours he came back with a man named John. They laughed like kids and old friends as they exchanged stories and sipped their drinks for the next few hours.

When John left, we asked, "Who was that man?" Dad just laughed and told us that he had just had an 'accidental' meeting with John. As he was driving along, obviously daydreaming, he had run into the rear end of John's car. That was the only explanation we could get out of him before he broke into laughter again about the whole incident.

We grew up in a small valley off the beaten path. Half a mile behind our back porch was a lake. We loved to fish and went down to the lake with our fishing poles several times a week. We were healthy boys with dark hair and eyes, curious natures and both good athletes, so every season meant a different sports activity.

Adam and I became known by our mischievous behavior. We would chase Megan our neighbor or wait behind a bush or in a ditch until she came by so we could jump out and scare her. I'm not sure if our neighbors ever really understood our antics and mischief, but I guess they learned to tolerate it as the years passed.

Even in school our arrival each day alerted teachers, janitors, and all the students that trouble was on the scene. Our stunts were never destructive or dangerous. It just felt good to stir things up, and besides, I'm sure we knew on some level that our father would always be there to iron things out. His visits signaled to everyone that we had done something wrong again. The worst punishment that we received was detention after school, but I feel sure that was due entirely to Dad's skill in diplomacy and advocacy for his two sons who had lost their mother so long ago.

Fifteen years of living, and yet I had to struggle to recall these few happy experiences. *What a shame*, I thought, but what really hit me was, *What a waste*.

On a very warm July day, Adam and I decided to go bass fishing on the lake. Armed with our rods, bait, lotion, cooler, and bathing trunks, we headed toward the lake. We knew it was too hot to catch any fish at eighty-seven degrees in the shade, but it was a perfect day to lay back and take it easy.

We got into the boat with a full tank of gas and took off across the lake keeping pretty close to the shore. We laughed about the girls we had met the day before while our lines drifted along side the boat. Then Adam decided to dive into the warm water.

"Wait, let me pull my line in and drop the anchor," I was saying. But Adam, who was by nature always impatient and liked to be first at everything, dove right in. He never knew what hit him and died instantly when his head hit the tree stump just below the surface of the water.

I don't remember the rescue or how I got to the shore. I guess I blocked certain parts out completely. In one split second the brother I loved so completely was gone.

The next month was grim — to say the least. Overwhelming feelings of pain, sadness, and grief erupted uncontrollably rendering a vacuum in my mind so that I still don't remember the wake and funeral of my twin brother. My father and I ceased living and moved into a routine of painful existence. Life, as I had experienced it, had been put on the back burner, and my future had been changed forever.

I guess our neighbors occasionally checked in on us because we were too out of touch to take care of things, and really didn't care anyway. Dad took Adam's death very hard, and this man who had once believed in positive thinking made no effort to shake himself out of his private grief. He grew more and more into himself and seldom talked to anyone. His wonderful sense of humor left and was replaced with anger, impatience, and insomnia.

I was just as hurt, and for the first time in my life my father refused to talk to me. After a while my sadness changed to resentment. Yes, he had lost a son, but I had lost my best pal — someone who always knew what I was thinking, and lots of times said it to me before I got the words out of my mouth. From the beginning we had done everything together, and suddenly — he was gone. Dad never said a word of blame, but I felt his eyes on my back which felt like cold, steel blades piercing my heart.

Being fifteen years old, losing my twin brother, feeling the blame from my own father and the guilt that I inflicted upon myself, it took less than six months for Dad and I to cease all communications. The loss of Adam was too great for both of us to talk about. He was becoming a stranger to me, and I felt like a boarder in his house, no more.

One evening I went to sleep, which was no small affair in the state of mind I was in during those days. I considered it a bonus to drift off to sleep for even a nap anytime of the day or night. Suddenly I was awake sitting in the middle of the bed shaking, soaked in my sweat and my heart pounding out of control. *It wasn't a dream nor was it a nightmare*, I thought. I panicked. I didn't know what had happened. All I knew was that I felt totally paralyzed by a frightening feeling that gripped me and wouldn't let go. Slowly I began to remember —

I had dreamed of this place that I could only describe as a void. I couldn't feel anything. I mean nothing. No joy, no pain — all feeling vanished. It was as if someone had yanked out my heart and everything with it. It was eerie. My heart felt empty, and I felt like a child who had to learn everything over again when I awoke.

After that episode I didn't sleep for four nights. I would doze during the day, but the nights absolutely terrified me. Every time I did actually sleep at night I would remember the void and knew that slowly, but surely, my memories were disappearing. Gone were my memories of my childhood, school, church, trips, and laughter. They were replaced by fear, rage, and anger. I couldn't think of anything good or happy that had occurred in my life.

These feelings got so bad that I refused to sleep at night entirely. I napped during the day and became more and more agitated, dreading the dark. To top things off, my father who was no longer my father, kicked me out.

In my anger after the last confrontation with him I had thumbed my way to the city. There I was, fifteen, and on the street. No parents, no skills, no place to live, no memories, no money, and scared out of my wits every time it got dark. I'll never forget that first night. The security of my home was gone, I had no bed to call my own, and all familiar sights and sounds had changed to new and threatening ones. These thoughts didn't come immediately but over the course of the long night. By dawn, all I had from thinking was a massive headache and a fierce hunger. I still had no answers to the numerous questions that kept popping into my head, but it seemed vital to hold on to the bits and pieces left to keep myself going.

I was still pondering recent events when I became aware of the flow of traffic around me, and the noise revived me a little. Spying a restaurant across the street I headed over to it, entered and found a booth in the back. I was in no hurry. I had all the time in the world in front of me and no clue of what I was going to do next.

After ordering a hamburger and a soda, I found myself looking around the place observing the activities of the people working there. The bartender behind the bar with his sleeves rolled up moved with ease as he grabbed the frosty mugs with one hand and longnecks in the other. A waitress was yelling in an order to the line cook while a busboy meticulously wiped the table that he had just cleaned off.

None of this felt real, and I felt like a little boy visiting in a strange place. I counted out the money for my bill and stood up and walked over to the jukebox putting in my last quarter. I pushed a button — any button, it really didn't matter. A CD flipped out of the stack and was placed in the player. A tejano melody floated out of the jukebox pretty loudly.

The music immediately took me away as I returned to my booth. I found myself staring outside at a lone cactus growing in a pot near the entrance. For just a moment I was in an open field feeling the wind in my face with the crunch of dry grass under my feet.

"Do you need a refill?" her voice snapped me out of my dream.

"Yes, please," I sat in the restaurant for quite some time watching the flow. Finally, I got up and left and walked the streets until it started to drizzle. *Great, what next?*

I found a little alcove surrounding an old forgotten doorway. It seemed as if it had been boarded up for at least twenty years. The hours crawled by. The oppression of the weather and my fear of the night was magnified as the cold began to sink in, beginning with my feet and working its way up my whole body.

The drizzle continued. After a while I became numb to it and couldn't feel anything. What was I doing here curled up in a cold dark corner like a beaten dog? I could not and would not sleep. All my muscles were stiff.

The drizzle stopped and was replaced by a bitterly cold wind. I could tell it was from the north, and it hit me like a whip. I felt the life in my body start up again if only to shiver against the cold. It was dawn. Never had I been so glad to see the light of day.

I forced myself from the corner I had adopted as my bedroom. When I stood up I had the distinct impression of my bones creaking like dry timber. Ouch, I was stiff. Little did I know how tough the next couple nights were going to be. I was cold, I was hungry, and I was in a city I had visited maybe ten times in my life. The next few days I walked endlessly through the streets. A menacing feeling constantly hung over my head.

I had stumbled past a donation box and added another shirt and sweater to my wardrobe, but the shivering which had become a part of me came from deep within. Not knowing what I was looking for I instinctively knew that I had to keep moving. I found water occasionally from spigots in the alleyways but couldn't bring myself to rummage through the smelly garbage. By the third day I did try begging out of desperation.

With my hand reaching in the direction of a passing stranger, "Do you have some spare change?"

"No," each person said, the same thing again and again as they hurried by avoiding even looking at me. *When you live in a parallel world, one might as well be invisible*, I thought.

One morning I was sitting in my home in a deserted alley between broken cardboard boxes and torn garbage bags. Too weak to move, with the smell of rotting food all around me making my empty stomach churn, I must have fallen into a stupor because the next thing I remember was hearing something whirling above my head. I thought, *What is going on?*

I looked up, and there was this bird. The flapping of his wings had brushed my head. I could tell the bird was hungry and wanted to rest like me. I didn't want to scare him so I kept very still as he hopped around on the pavement without ever noticing me.

The listlessness engulfed me again, but the welts and blisters on my feet kept me from falling asleep. The pain was excruciating. This, added to the despair from the cold, hunger, and nightmares that haunted me night after night, had me pretty beaten down. This was definitely a new game with nondescript rules.

Amazingly, my pride was still intact, which made going back home out of the question, and it was about all I had to hold onto for the moment. But I was slowly conscious of a thought that kept returning to my mind, *Help me*! *Somebody help me*!

On the fourth day of wandering the streets with no prospects, a scream jolted me out of my absorbed mind. I looked around. The neighborhood was deserted except for the litter. Down the street was an old, empty movie theater. Between the ticket box office and entry doors I saw two shapes. As I walked closer, I could make out two kids shouting at each other.

The bigger kid was obviously bullying the small guy, pushing him up against the door. Suddenly he started shaking him like a willow tree and banging his head against an oversized chain and padlock on the cinema doors.

When the victim saw me, he instinctively shouted out, "Help me, Doug, for god's sake!" The bully jumped back like a startled cat caught with the canary. He dropped the fellow and swung around, looked me right in the eye and automatically decided it wasn't worth it. He turned and ran off like a wild rabbit, never stopping until he was out of sight.

"Hey, man, sorry I called you Doug. It's all I could think of at the moment. My name is Tony. What's yours?" asked this kid still crumpled on the sidewalk.

"Alex."

"Well, Alex, thanks for helping me," Tony said as he picked himself up off the concrete. A trickle of blood was running from behind his ear, and a glob of spit ran down his chin. He was shaking as badly as

I was.

When Tony stood up I got a better look at him. Man, was he dirty and smelly. He was scrawny and his clothes were tattered, but he had a look of defiance on his face. He looked younger than me with grubby, ash blonde hair and some chipped teeth. What was most peculiar was that he had only one eye. The other one was covered with an old black patch as dirty as his clothes.

"Do you have some spare change?" not missing a beat as he was dusting himself off.

"No, I left my last quarter in a jukebox a few days ago."

"Yeah, right. You're all dressed up, clean, and you're going to tell me you ain't got no money? Don't give me that bull."

"No, I swear. My dad kicked me out four days ago, and I don't even remember how I got here. I've been sleeping in the streets, wandering around, drinking out of spigots in alleys. I've got nothing. You've got to believe me," I was begging.

"Okay, okay. I believe you."

"I don't know where to go," I admitted. Tony stunk, but since he was alive he must know something about survival. I had to trust someone.

"Welcome to the streets, man. First, call me One Eye. Everyone else calls me that," he added with a hint of a smile.

"You got it, whatever you say."

"Second, stop shrinking your nose at me. After two or three weeks you'll have the same stink," he said, starting to act tough again.

"Me? Never." I wasn't ever going to smell that bad.

"Wanna bet?"

"Bet with what?" as I showed him my empty pockets, turning them inside out.

"Hey. Stop with the 'poor me.' You helped me, I'll help you." Tony, I mean One Eye, saw our situation that simply.

"Lucky me," trying to sound tough like him.

"Hey! Smart, clean guy, have it your way. It's rough out here. Don't waste time. Follow me if you want. It's no skin off my back," talking as he turned down an alley behind some warehouses, stray cats running away from him.

I needed all the help I could get. So I hurried behind, "Tony, where did you say you live?"

"I told you, call me One Eye. Actually I didn't say, but you'll see if you can keep up." Tony was proud of his "home." Last winter he discovered a crawl space on the roof over the print shop. It was fine for one person to get out of the rain and cold up against the AC unit. Piece by piece he accumulated lumber in the middle of the night and enlarged the area for a couple of his friends. It was noisy, but warm and dry, and secure from the street.

"Man, I could have used it last night. That drizzle soaked me to the bone, and I shivered all night."

"What do you mean last night? You're still shivering. Hurry up, Alex, we gotta get some different clothes for you, or they won't believe you're homeless down at the shelter."

With blisters on my blisters I was going as fast as I could, "Not so fast. My feet are killing me — I haven't taken my shoes off in five days."

"That will be an event to miss, but I'm not about to skip a meal — so move it!"

"I'm coming, you sarcastic weasel," was all I could muster at the moment.

He didn't even bother to reply. He was already twenty feet ahead, silently gliding by the building walls. We turned left behind a great big dumpster which concealed a narrow alleyway.

"Normally I don't come here during the daytime, but you look too clean in your clothes. Don't make any noise." One Eye looked nervously around the alley.

A rope which ran alongside the wall was covered by some trash. One Eye pulled with his whole frail body. Suddenly, it happened. The rusty fire escape came down with ease.

"Hop on it," he hissed.

I literally flew up the wall to the roof. "Hey, neat. No one will find us up here."

"Shut up," he whispered.

Once we were on the top of the roof, One Eye stopped. He looked around and proceeded to walk toward a small shed covering the AC. He went in, and I followed. To my surprise this place was warm and cozy and also full of junk.

"What is all that stuff?" I asked.

"It's how I make my living. Over in that box is everything you need. Sneakers, jeans, radios, blankets, t-shirts, toys, socks, shoes, pants, and a lot more." One Eye showed me around with a touch of pride.

"Where did you get all this stuff?" was my next question.

"People leave things in boxes for the homeless at the shelter and drop-boxes. I have no home so that makes it legal, right?" he reasoned.

Boy, this kid was smart. I'm lucky I met him. A friend, shelter, clothes, and the possibility of a meal, all wrapped up in one skinny package. I picked a shirt, a pair of pants, and some sneakers. When I had changed, he said, "Let's go eat."

We took the fire escape down. I felt good. I was dry, and the future looked better already. Imagine, one hour ago I was freaking out. At the mission everyone had been there and left.

Tony waved madly at a woman who was closing the door. "Hey, Peggy! Wait! My friend and I need to eat."

"Tony, how come you're so late?" a middle-aged woman with light hair asked. She looked tired but kind, her question showing concern rather than a gripe.

"Got held up. What's left?" One Eye asked.

"I got chicken, roast potatoes, corn, and bread, of course," she rattled off the menu for a feast from what I heard. "Who's the new kid?"

"Alex. He helped me this morning. Rick was trying to kick my butt when Alex showed up as my friend. He scared Rick off, and the jerk ran away like a whipped puppy." He put a hand on my shoulder and smiled his jagged smile.

"Hi, Alex. I'm Peggy. Sit down, and I'll fix you up. Hot tea is all we've got left to drink." She smiled at us and went back to the kitchen area.

"Good enough," I replied. The smell of real, safe, warm food made my stomach rumble like thunder, and I felt weak with starvation. *Just a few more minutes*, I told myself.

We sat on some folding chairs while Peggy prepared two plates piled high with food. It was the most beautiful sight I had ever seen.

"It's ready," she finally announced.

I jumped out of my seat and grabbed the plate from her hands. I quickly sat down at the table and began to wolf down the food. One Eye acted more cool and gave a little laugh while he watched me.

"Slow down," Peggy said. "If you haven't eaten in awhile, you'll get sick eating like that. Take your time. Nobody's gonna steal the food."

She was right. Halfway through my plate I had to stop so I wouldn't throw up. I stopped for a moment and took a sip of tea, and let my stomach acknowledge that, yes, this was real food. After fifteen minutes the wave of sickness had passed, and I could take another bite. I was going to make it after all.

"You look happy," One Eye smiled, but this time giving me his best chipped-tooth grin.

My mouth was full, my stomach getting there, and looking at my new buddy, I answered, "Best meal I've had in quite a while. Thanks."

Familiarizing myself with the neighborhood over the next few days, learning the ins and outs of the streets and alleys, I discovered that this neighborhood had a lot of poverty. Most of the people living here were doing only a tiny bit better than One Eye and me on the streets. Almost all of the cars in the streets that were still running were at least ten years old, if not older.

I heard footsteps coming up behind me. I turned to look and got punched in the nose. A symphony of stars appeared in my head.

"Remember me, you stupid punk?" the voice said. I was flat on the ground. I opened my eyes to see Rick, the bully, this time with three of his friends. Blood was pouring from my nose. I had better not let them see how scared I was.

"Oh, hey, it's you. The moron. What's up?" I asked.

With no warning all four guys started beating the crap out of me, kicking me between the punches. I tried to fight back, but there were too many of them. I curled up to protect my head as my only defense, before I gratefully passed out from the pain.

When I came to, I realized those idiots had left me for dead between some stinking garbage bags in a slimy gutter. Even though I was conscious, I couldn't move. I was beaten to a pulp and retching from the pain. *I could die here, and no one would even know to tell my dad*, I thought half-heartedly. Then I lost track of time once again.

It was already dark when One Eye and his pal Jack found me.

They told me how it took them forever to drag me up the fire escape and into the hideaway, though I don't remember any of this. One Eye also told me how delirious I was, going on and on about some void and the nightmare which sucked out my memory.

He nursed my injuries the best that he could for three days and fed me soup that he had gotten from Peggy. He also brought some bread, but apparently my lips were so swollen that liquids were all that I could handle. For the first time since my brother died, I had a friend and that felt very special to me.

One day I was lying curled up against the air conditioner listening to the motor purring. I was thinking about the rage of the guys that had beaten me up, when I noticed something out of the corner of my swollen eye. At first it seemed like just a mist in the corner of the shed, but as I sat there and watched, it actually took form — kinda like a human shadow. I dismissed it as my imagination or better yet delirium from my injuries. But then the form whirled around me a couple of times. I watched in awe. It became still for a moment, then disappeared.

Talk about being unnerved and rattled, I must have been hit harder in the head than I thought. The shadow had startled me, but it wasn't scary or threatening. It almost had a friendly feeling about it. Definitely different from the nightmares that had returned with a vengeance since my injuries. Sleeping at night had become out of the question with the void sucking my memories at an ever increasing rate. My childhood was vanishing bit by bit with less to hang on to every day.

I finally went outside after seven or eight days, and experiencing the wind in my hair and sun on my face felt good. Feeling alive again made me smile through my pain.

One Eye showed me how to commit my first crime. We went to the back door of a small produce store. One Eye grabbed a trash can and, with all the strength in his skinny body, threw it against the back door.

Of course, the owner wondered what the hell all the noise was and came back to investigate. While he was checking out the noise in the back, One Eye and I ran up front into the store and grabbed a couple of apples. Our *crime* was accomplished in a few seconds.

We ventured down to another corner store, and this time Bill was with us. He had less trouble lifting a full trash can and flinging it at the door. We all ran up and grabbed some fruit when the owner went back to check on the noise.

All three of us took off running, down the alley and through the narrow passages, leaping over trash cans like crazy. We were gone before anyone knew what had happened. We all came to a stop at the same time. The uneven pavement was rough under our feet. My heart was pounding, trying to leap out of my chest. What a rush! We trembled, we laughed, jumping up for high five exchanges.

After we calmed down and ate the apples, I started to feel a little guilty. I knew that what we had done was wrong, dead wrong. But, I had this other feeling as well. It's hard to describe, but it was the only real sensation I had experienced since the terror of my nightmares had started. I felt like I was here and could feel the blood flowing through my veins. After that, the rules of society became irrelevant when it came to surviving on the streets. Staying alive and taking care of your buddies were the basic rules of the street.

One particularly grim morning I was still walking around after wandering the streets all night. I was feeling especially sorry for myself, walking down the dark alley, looking at the holes in my shoes, in no rush to get anywhere. At the corner I collided with a stranger.

"Hey! What's the hurry, young man?" he asked.

"Who wants to know?" I had learned from One Eye to act tough with everybody. That way, no one would think you were a wimp.

"No need to give me lip. After all, you bumped into me."

"Yeah? Sue me!" I started walking away.

"Hey, wait. What's your name?"

"Who wants to know?" It was strange having a grownup ask my name. To most of the public, I was just a smelly, faceless piece of trash.

"Simon, that's who wants to know. My name is Simon. What, you don't know your name?" He was following me into the street.

"Hey, watch it. Besides, why do you care?" Why was he so interested? Bill had told me about scummy guys who were selling drugs to street kids and others who would try to make kids have sex with them. No way was I going to fall into those traps.

"Chill out. You look like you could use a cup of coffee."

"You buying?" If he tried anything, at least I could throw hot coffee in his face was my thinking.

"Sure, you pick a place," he answered, which coming from even a stranger sounded safe enough.

"You include a donut with the coffee?" You don't get it if you don't ask — another rule of the street.

"Can do."

"You're on, and Alex is the name." I figured a hot breakfast was worth telling him my first name.

Looking at this man, I noticed that he was tall and slender with rough hands. His pants were fairly old with baggy knees. He had a small mole on the right side of his neck, just below his chin. His tie was nothing special and his shoes were old. He had brown hair that he had pulled back and secured, and he had at least a three-day beard. It only took me half a second to size him up. He definitely wasn't rolling in the dough. There was something peculiar about his eyes, but I brushed the thought away.

"Alex, pleased to meet you."

"Yeah, yeah, what about the donut and hot java?"

"Hey, take it easy," he said with a smile. "Do you know a place around here?"

"There's a place up the block good enough for coffee. Let's go." He and I didn't say another word until we sat down in a booth.

"Tell me," we said at the same time and then laughed.

"Go ahead," said Simon.

"No, you go first."

"What will it be guys?" Maggie the waitress had snuck up on us. She winked at me. She had given me coffee from time to time when

I was broke or cold, which was just about all the time.

"A coffee, two donuts, and lots of cream," Simon ordered.

"Same for me." Smiling to myself. Wow! An extra donut and hot coffee for breakfast!

The next few minutes were spent in uneasy silence. I didn't mind. It was a free breakfast.

I broke the silence, "So, what brings you to this neck of the woods?"

"Actually, I've been looking for you the last four days."

I made a motion to get up and split. Someone looking for you always meant trouble, cops or someone looking for revenge, or worse.

"Hey, slow down and let me explain." Simon said.

"I don't even know you. Why were you looking for me?" still standing ready to bolt at one wrong word or movement.

"One Eye and Jack told me about you."

Nobody had said that they were trying to connect me with anyone. "How do I know that I can trust you?" I continued.

"Butterball said you were the best at stealing cars."

"Butterball?" If this guy was a cop, I had better play dumb. "Who's Butterball?"

"You know very well who Butterball is," he snapped.

"No, I don't."

This guy was really persistent. "Yes, you do. His real name is John. When he was four years old his mom put the Thanksgiving turkey on the top of the stove after taking it out of the oven. John tried to check out what was smelling so good and pulled the turkey on top of himself, splashing hot grease all over him and leaving a huge scar on his forehead."

That was his nickname, but very few people knew the real story. In the twilight of misery, no explanation is necessary in the streets. If Simon knew about Butterball, maybe he could be trusted. But he still made me nervous. I sat back down.

"Who are you, exactly?" I finished the question just as Maggie brought the donuts and coffee. Waiting for his answer I started making them disappear.

"I told you, Simon."

"So, but what else? What do you do?" His eyes kept annoying me. Icy, mean, and downright conniving. Again, I put my intuition on a back burner ignoring the warning signs.

Simon waited until Maggie was behind the counter again. "I 'recycle' hot cars."

"Oh. That Simon. We call you Ghost."

"Ghost it is then," Simon acknowledged.

Ghost started trying to persuade me to steal cars for him. I was long past feeling guilty for committing crimes to survive, so I listened. After I told him I would never have anything to do with drugs, he outlined a plan that would make some money for both of us.

At the beginning, I got some impressive money by street standards for my skills, and other street kids wanted to jump on the gravy train. Soon Ghost had a small army of kids picking pockets, shoplifting, stealing cars, whatever — whatever crime Ghost could think up to get the profits from and still keep his own butt out of jail. It was understood that he would get us out of jail if needed, but I never knew anyone who called him on it. We were streetwise and didn't count on anyone except our buddies. Some kids did act like slaves to him and thought that they needed him to take care of them.

But no matter how much of his dirty work we did, his plans never got anyone off the streets.

I lost track of the outside world. No radio, newspapers, or TV. Not that I really cared, but when I heard about politics, or a new car, or new song it was already old to everyone else. Mostly I slept during the day and beat the pavement at night. The nightmares persisted and that shadow form kept appearing from time to time, never distinctly, but always at the most inopportune times, always without warning.

If it hadn't been for One Eye, I don't know how I would've survived. I don't think I would have made it. Jack was a great friend, too. He was big and strong and didn't take crap from anyone. Then there was Butterball. He was a little slow in everything that he did, but he knew every trick when it came to finding a place to hide or how to locate a shelter or food. He was constantly looking for us a better place to live.

Finally, he found an abandoned building. We could enter through a manhole size opening, squeeze around these huge pipes, and then walk down a hallway into a big room. We covered the floor with flattened cardboard boxes, stacking three or four to create our beds. One Eye's stuff was piled in a corner. There were plenty of blankets and brick pillows, and more than enough room for the four of us. The roof didn't leak, and that made it all the more easier to keep warm in the winter and cool in the sizzling summer heat.

We did some crazy things in that time, but we all agreed that drugs were off-limits. We even took an oath that we would never do drugs. The money we made barely fed us, let alone wasting it on chemical garbage. We had no leader, we just stuck together somehow. When an idea came up, we all talked about it and developed a plan to achieve it.

One day Jack and I were looking for something to do when we saw this kid. He had a hole in one of his sneakers, only one shoelace, his shirt half tucked in, and was trembling from the cold. Probably no food in his stomach. He looked like one of us.

"Slept outside, I reckon," Jack said to him.

"Yeah, man, what a bummer. I nearly froze my butt off. I covered myself with cardboard." He talked really fast.

There was something about him that interested me. "My name is Alex, and this guy is Jack. What's your name?"

"Randy, but everyone calls me Lips."

"Lips. Why Lips?" I asked before I thought.

"Cause I never shut up."

"Where are you from?" Jack asked.

"Small town in South Dakota." Wow, this kid was a long way from home, and couldn't be over fourteen or fifteen.

"What are you doing so far from home?" I continued.

"Nothing better to do. Besides my parents died in a car crash when I was nine years old. None of the family wanted me, so I got sent to the state slime pit and then a bunch of foster homes. Those foster homes suck. Man, the kids pick on you, and the grownups are just in it for the check. No one cares. One day I got fed up and took off as soon as I could and ended up here," he rattled on.

"Hold on. Slow down. You do talk fast — you're making my

head spin. Want something to eat? I've got seventy-eight cents," as I checked my change. "What've you got, Jack?"

"Don't know, let me look," as Jack started going through his pockets. "Three dollars and four cents. Man, we're rich! Let's get soup and bread and share it with the others. Come on, Randy."

Back at the building, Bill warmed up the soup in a pot he had found in some garbage can in a residential neighborhood and a sterno can that he had found behind a restaurant. We all ate out of the pot with our plastic spoons. Randy was so hungry that he wiped the pot clean with his bread.

"When was the last time you ate?" asked Butterball.

"Four days ago. That's when I ran away."

As the afternoon wore on, we all realized at the same time that Lips could talk your ears off. He knew lots of things about politics, cars, boats, cats, building houses, countries, and even mountains. All he did for five years was read to escape the foster parents that the state imposed on him. Sometimes one of us had to tell him to shut up.

Jack made a little room in a corner with a couple of extra blankets. "Hey, Lips. Get over here and don't say another word."

Lips got up and went over to Jack and looked in the corner.

"Here's your bed. Two blankets and a brick for a pillow. If you want to fancy it up, I'll give you another brick. That's all the comfort we can give you." Jack smiled at our noisy new friend.

"Hey guys, thanks! Thanks a lot."

"Now go with One Eye. He's the store keeper."

One Eye grabbed him by the arm and led him to his corner in the next room. Lips was so happy to have found some new friends, he would have gone anywhere with us without question. "Here, take whatever you want. There are clothes, shoes, socks, and lots more. Knock yourself out."

Digging through the stack, Lips looked like a kid in a toy store. "Man, you've got everything here. This is a big building. What do we do about washing and using the bathroom?"

One Eye explained that the public library had a restroom by the entrance and that the employees didn't seem to care if we used it as long as we went in one by one. "Go ahead and change after you find what you need. I'll wait on you in the next room."

As he turned to leave, One Eye remembered the most important rule, "If you need something else, ask first. I'll get it. There's a lot of other kids out there that are in needs. We take care of each other."

We were all waiting when One Eye came and sat down with us, "Everybody comfortable with Lips?"

"Seems okay," Butterball answered.

Jack put his hands over his ears, but shook his head up and down, as Bill gave his approval.

"Well, I guess he's in."

After a minute of quiet I broke the silence, "Jack and I spent all our money for lunch."

"That's cool. I was planning to beg on the corner of Main and Ruston Street," said One Eye. "With one eyeball out, women have pity on me and give me more money than the men."

"I'll come with you to keep a lookout." Bill offered. "I heard that Rick is hanging out near there."

Jack jumped to his feet. "Well, I need to go and teach that bully some manners." He started popping his knuckles and flexing his muscles.

"Hold on a moment, Jack, sit down. We don't need to start a fight. Our life is complicated enough, let me talk to him," I said hoping to keep him out of trouble. Jack was about the strongest guy on the street and our protector, like big brother, but his quick temper stirred up problems sometimes before there was a problem.

"Alex, you're kidding. He beat you up and left you for dead, and you want to talk to that scum?" One Eye reminded me.

"That's why I should go," said Jack. "If he touches one hair on your head, he's blending with the pavement."

"Deal, but give me one chance to talk to him," as I laughed at Jack's shadow boxing antics.

Lips appeared in the doorway standing in his new clothes with his old rags under his arm, "What do I do with these?"

Nobody answered him. We were all looking at him — sports shirt, slacks, and a jean jacket made him totally presentable.

"Frame them for the memories," Bill joked.

"No, we dump them," I said.

"Whatever. If you and Jack are going with One Eye, then I guess I'll head out to work." Bill turned to leave for his job delivering groceries. It was low pay, but the boss' wife knew his situation and always gave him ripe fruit and packages of stuff about to expire to compensate. Besides, the tips were usually decent, and he got to clean up at the store.

I got up to leave with One Eye a couple of minutes later when Lips spoke up, "What about me?"

"Right, I forgot. Come with us or crash here if you want. But if you go out alone, be sure no one follows you. We don't need a city slicker investigating this building. It's too comfortable to lose it. And if you want to hang out with us, then you have to stay away from drugs. We already have enough ways to get killed or busted." I wanted to be sure that he understood the rules of the house.

"No problem. I saw too many space cadets in those foster homes, I don't want to be a druggie. I'll be careful when I leave, but for now I think I'll just hang here and sleep." Lips got the picture and obviously felt at home.

"See you later, Lips." He had joined our family.

One Eye and I left the building and walked across our bad section of town to an area with more people and money. It was finally starting to warm up, the sun was shining and it only took about twenty minutes to reach Main and Ruston Street. The street was packed with swarms of people.

"Too many folks," was my opinion.

But One Eye saw it differently, "Leave it up to me. This corner is a money maker."

"Okay, I'll watch." I didn't want Rick sneaking up on me again, that was for sure, but mostly I didn't see the point in one street kid getting beat up by another. Maybe he'd listen to reason.

It took me less than five seconds to spot Rick half a block down, soaking up the sun with two of his buddies. For me, there was only one thing to do, just walk right up to him with all the confidence in the world, shield myself with energy, and let go of all the anger and fear. Positive energy counters negative energy. *Where did that thought come from?* I wondered for a moment.

Self assurance always disconcerts the opposition, was my last thought as I approached Rick and his buddies. "Hey, Rick. Soaking up the sun?"

"Now, look who's here. Come after another fat lip?" Rick and his pals got to their feet and started trying to look tough. They all looked at me like my days were numbered.

"Take it easy," I said trying to keep my voice cool and confident.

"Why should I? I can whip you any day, so scram." Rick moved toward me and motioned to his buddies who backed off a few steps.

"I just came to talk," I continued.

"Talk about what, rich kid? How to keep pretending you're having a hard life?" he snarled.

Had he beaten me up because he thought I was rich? "What do you mean, rich kid?"

"Cut the crap. You know what I'm talking about. I've been asking around, and so have your dad's company people." Rick caught me off guard with that last statement.

"Well, if you've been asking around, you know I'm from a small town, and I haven't gone back once since my dad kicked me out. I didn't need his rules anymore," I said, but I was wondering if my dad had really been looking for me.

"Kicked you out? Bull! You're just spying, probably working for the cops or something." Rick sat down on an empty crate pushing his long dirty hair out of his face.

"Oh, yeah, I just love sleeping on cardboard, wearing dirty clothes, walking around with an empty stomach, and I especially like smelling like a wet dog all day and constantly looking over my shoulder for guys like you. Man, this is the rich kid's life, for sure," I sarcastically shot back.

"Yeah, yeah, you're good man — good at faking it."

This was harder than I thought it would be. This guy is really sour on life. "Faking it? I can't look people in the eye, I'm so ashamed." It was hard telling this bully that I was ashamed, but it was true.

"That's crap!"

"My father kicked me out 'cause I couldn't sleep at night and slept most of the day, he thought I was just lazy, a bum." Maybe Rick could relate to getting kicked out.

"I heard about your wanderings at night and that imaginary shadow that haunts you. Man, you are nuts or crazy. Just get lost, weirdo." He turned away.

"Fine. Have it your way," I said as I started to leave.

Rick called me back, "All right, so maybe you're not rich,

_no...

maybe you're just a street bum like me. Why should we be friends?" For the first time he didn't sound so threatening.

Seizing the opportunity, I answered, "First of all, we all have enough problems in the street without creating more by fighting among ourselves. Second, I heard about you helping Peggy ward off an attacker as she came out of the shelter. I wanted to shake hands with a hero."

"You heard about that?" as his surprise spread across his face.

"Yeah, that's the word on the street."

"Well, she was getting mugged, and I just couldn't let it happen," he shrugged.

"That's what I mean. We have enough crap around us. That's why we need to take care of our own, and not waste time beating up each other. Street folks got to stick together, and you did great helping Peggy."

Rick smiled and flexed his chest like a proud peacock. He looked me right in the eye and said, "She's the only real person around us. She cares, and half the kids would starve if it wasn't for her."

I extended my hand, "So let's shake." Would he do it?

Rick put his hand in mine. All the animosity was gone. He had a look of pride and a twinkle in his eyes. "So you really heard?" he questioned, still finding it hard to believe.

"Yeah. We all think you're a hero," I smiled and felt truly relaxed for the first time.

"Stop it. You'll make me blush." Rick glanced back to see if his friends could hear us.

How strange it was to see this side of the street's toughest guy, "You? Blush? Get outta here," I said leaning toward him so no one could hear.

"Well, this is the first time anyone thought I did something good."

Jack snuck up on us swaggering like a tough guy. I stepped between Jack and Rick seeing Jack's desire to help me and said, "Everything's okay. We're just chatting about Rick helping Peggy last week."

Jack stammered, "Just checking on my pals. Let's go see if One Eye has struck it rich."

I reached out and gave another street shake to Rick. "See you around, Buddy," Rick responded and smiled. I grinned back at him knowing that things were definitely going to be better.

One Eye had been lucky. "Nine bucks in twenty minutes. I'm on a roll," he laughed.

"Gimme five, man. We'll go get donuts." Jack was always as hungry as Lips was talkative.

"All right, Jack, but I'm staying. Like I said, I'm on a roll. Bring me a jelly."

"Jelly, it is," said Jack as we headed down the street.

Every day in the street was a struggle. Most of the time it was hard, but it was never boring. In my next life I think I'll pick a better way to make it.

Very early one summer morning, just at the break of dawn, I came home from my nightly wanderings. I took off my shoes and t-shirt and got ready to lie down. Butterball and One Eye were sound asleep. It was then that the shadow appeared, more visible than ever, moving like crazy. I tried to dismiss it, but it got more agitated. Hell, it got down right aggressive.

"What do you want? Go away. You don't scare me!" Again, it just vanished.

At that precise moment Lips walked into the room. He moved like he was in a trance and entered as silently as a cloud. He was shaking like a leaf on a tree in the wind. He tripped over Bill's blanket and almost lost his balance. He steadied himself and stood perfectly still, not uttering a sound.

I couldn't really see him clearly because it was still dark, but I sensed something was wrong. He was just standing there, frozen in the dark.

"What's going on?" asked Butterball, rubbing his eyes.

"Don't know," said Bill, now awake too. "He tripped over me."

I jumped out of my bed like greased lightening, body hairs raised like a wild cat with the premonition of danger. I grabbed Lips by the shoulders. The panic was gaining on me. The shadow had just been an irritation or aggravation earlier. But now this?

"Talk to me, Lips. What's going on with you? You always talk. Talk now. Now is not the time to keep it inside."

Suddenly I realized that I was shaking him as hard as I could, then I just grabbed him in my arms holding on to him. Everybody was up now and scared out of their wits. I took a deep breath. It was not the time to panic. Just stay calm. I grabbed Lips on each side of his head and looked him square in the eyes. They were empty, vacant, and distant. Tears slid down his cheeks, and his mouth was quivering.

"Talk to me, Randy. What's going on with you? Snap out of it." By now the unknown was really overpowering me.

"Lips, don't let go. Talk. You know we love you, but for god's sake, snap out of it."

Man, he was like a zombie. What had put him in such a state of shock? I had to snap him out of it. I took him into my arms. The shadow reappeared just behind Lips. It remained perfectly still. But I began to feel an energy entering me — a peaceful strength — flowing through me to Lips.

The shadow slowly faded, but the room seemed filled with a soft light and a serene feeling.

First, Lips shook his head and just a whisper came out. Nobody could hear it but me. His voice was incoherent at first, but after a few times the words came out clear enough to understand. They chilled me to the bone.

"He's dead, he's dead, he's dead, he's dead..." Lips kept

repeating this phrase like a broken record, and by now tears were pouring out of his eyes.

"Okay, Randy, calm down. Who's dead? I can't help you if you don't tell me what's going on."

He looked at me like he was in a dream. "It's too late, Alex, he's dead."

"Who? Where? What happened? I don't understand. Say something." By now the terror was giving me cramps in my stomach. I couldn't swallow. The rest of the gang was panicked, to say the least.

"Out there behind the old bakery, he's lying there in blood."

"Who? Tell me."

"He's dead! Jack's dead!"

I didn't need to hear any more. I ran the four and a half blocks in record time. I ran around the corner behind the bakery, then jolted to a full stop. Tears were in my eyes. Jack was laying in Simon's arms.

"I called an ambulance," said Ghost.

Jack was alive, but barely. His chest hardly moved, his eyes were glassy.

I knelt down beside him and told him to hang on. With all the strength left in him, he lifted his arm and pulled my head to his lips. He whispered a word in my ear, and then died quietly in Simon's arms.

In the background we could hear the siren of the ambulance getting closer. My anger was overwhelming.

"You did this! You used your influence and pushed him to steal cars and steal jewelry. Go away! Don't touch him!" I screamed.

Simon just looked at me. "Calm down. You're upset."

"Upset? You idiot, I said don't touch him!"

Simon eased Jack's body onto the pavement as the ambulance pulled up with its tires squealing. I didn't want to wait. I took off and left Simon to deal with the body and the barrage of questions that would follow.

Jack was dead. Dead. I was too shocked to register anything else in my mind. What Jack had whispered to me didn't make any sense. The word kept coming back to me, "Simon."

I know he died in his arms, but why Simon? Was he the last guy he recognized or wanted to make right with or what? And why had he pulled me to his lips to say that word as his last?

"Simon." It didn't make any sense. I panicked. Just the night before Jack and I had talked and laughed, and now my life once again came to a screeching halt. Everyone reacted mostly with denial to the violence we saw and experienced.

"The streets are dangerous," we had been telling each other, but we didn't really want to acknowledge it.

I got mad. How could he be dead? We all got used to his coming and going, sometimes disappearing for days at a time. At times he had been hiding, other times he had been in jail for petty theft or something minor. We could usually find out where he was through the other street kids. I remember how we met. I was curled up in that AC shack above the print shop all beaten up. He never asked any questions, he had helped get me to safety and he was just like a big brother to all of us. I guess it was just his time to go. I didn't have the answers to all my questions. Nobody did.

I was walking around in a daze. The night was cold, and it was raining. Nothing mattered anymore. I just lost it. It must have been two or three days since I had eaten or slept. My mind was scattered. I had lost all concept of time, but it didn't matter. My stomach thought otherwise and brought me back to reality.

Where was I? The greyness made it hard to tell what time it was, and I had obviously just walked clear across the city. As a matter of fact, I was in a small suburb of the industrial part of the city.

I shook my head a couple of times. Boy, did it hurt. Having no food for so long made me dizzy. I was shaking like a hundred year old man. *This is humiliating. I gotta do something to get out of this funk.* Swell, I was talking to myself. What's next? Hallucinations?

It was this incident that got me off the street. I was slowly coming out of my altered state, and reality gaining a firm grip when I stumbled across a small fair. Lots of noise, strings of lights running around the outline of the ferris wheel and carousel. Neon lights flashed "Fun" wherever I turned. Hawkers cried out to come check out the thrills, promising their ride was the best. People were smiling, children were laughing, couples were holding hands and carrying the stuffed animals won for their sweethearts. The weather was warm, and it seemed as if no one had a worry in the world. I guess these people had worked hard for this day off to have fun.

All the lights, music, crowd, kids laughing, and people shouting put me in a rejuvenated mood. I stood right in front of a cotton candy stand. A light breeze gently caressed my face. I was drunk with the smell of this mountain of "sugar on a stick." A good crowd can be the best remedy when you are down and out.

I looked around me. If I picked someone's pocket, I was sure to get caught because I was too weak to run. I could already imagine two policemen running after me, grabbing me, and hauling my butt off to jail. No time to risk something crazy.

As I dismissed that thought, I found myself in front of the bumper car ride, looking at the electrified grid of wires above the kids' heads. The grid spit out fierce blue sparks. The cars were vivid in color and raced toward each other on the rubber floor, bumping into each

F r a n ç o i s   S i g r i s t

other amidst explosions of laughter and screams. It was exhilarating to watch.

The boss lady was at the cash register selling tickets and briefing everyone on the rules. "No pushing, no bad language, keep your hands and arms in the car. Don't get out of the car until you come to a complete stop and I say it's okay to get out."

All the kids nodded their heads. They understood. The line was pretty long, but constantly ebbed and flowed as a new wave ran to jump into the recently vacated cars.

Her assistant was tall and slender, and sad looking. He would jump from car to car before the ride started to collect tickets. He was as agile as a cat, leaping from one car to another without touching the floor beneath him. In one fluid effort, he would grab the tickets and rip them in half. He didn't waste a single motion, not even to glance at the floor, his eyes were already on the next customer waving their ticket.

I was about to leave this show of acrobatic prowess when something strange happened. Maybe it was the hunger that made me see sharper, allowing me to see something just before it happened. In any case, just as I turned to leave, I had a premonition, and it nailed me to the ground. I couldn't move and had to watch. I knew something terrible was about to happen.

At this moment, the young attendant was jumping off the last car. All the tickets were in his hands, but as he jumped, his foot missed the wooden platform. At the same time, the boss, not realizing what had happened, turned on the juice. Sparks started flying, and the cars started moving and one ran over the young attendant's leg. It all occurred in a

54

split second followed by a bloodcurdling scream.

The boss immediately turned off the power. People jumped onto the floor. The boss made his way through the crowd. The attendant was moaning from the pain, his ankle dangling like a wet rag. He was in so much pain, there was only one thing for him to do — pass out.

The lady at the cash register grabbed the phone to call for help. One first aid person who wanted to help was already fighting his way through the crowd, but there was nothing he could do.

The ambulance arrived within minutes. Two paramedics came through the crowd with their bags in hand. They knelt beside the young man, and one proceeded to wrap the young man's ankle to secure it. The other one checked his vital signs for shock.

The young man regained consciousness. He grimaced from the pain. The police were asking questions about what had happened. The lady was closing the cash box, and the crowd was beginning to thin out. The paramedics lifted the poor guy after strapping him on a stretcher. The owner wasn't too happy.

"Honey," the cash register lady said to the owner, "What are we going to do?"

"I don't know. I guess I'll run the ride myself and take tickets. I'll lose one turn for every four, but that's better than closing."

"All right. I'll go open the register."

"You do that," he said, returning to the main control.

"Hey, boss," I called as I waved my hand to get his attention.

He looked at me and turned around walking away from me. Guess he had experienced enough trouble to waste time on a bum-looking kid.

"It's bad, isn't it?" getting his attention again.

Not looking at me he answered, "Yes. Broken leg, but it could've been worse."

"Hey, six weeks in a cast and he'll be as good as new," I was trying to sound positive.

"Six weeks. Sure, but in five weeks the season will be over."

I tucked in my shirt and asked, "Do you have somebody to replace him?"

"No, but I'll do it myself in the meantime." He still hadn't looked at me closely.

"Listen. I watched your helper. It didn't look too hard to me. I can do the same, except break my leg, of course," I said.

For the first time he turned and looked at me. I wasn't a great sight. I had a ten-day beard, I was dirty, I looked more like a hobo than a street hood. Plus, I probably smelled pretty ripe. When you live in an abandoned building you never look like the model on the cover of a magazine.

"Look, boss. A bar of soap and a razor blade will make me look human again, I promise. The name's Alex."

"Okay, Alex, I'll take you on a trial basis." He was giving me a chance. "Don't forget, in five weeks the season is over. You get $225 a week — plus room and board. Okay?"

"Great. I'll take it." *What a break*, oops, *I mean opportunity*, I thought.

"Now look here. All you have to do is collect the tickets as fast as you can. Take your time until you get the hang of it" He shook his head as he walked off.

I was tired, but happy I had just gotten a job. I went right to it, jumping on those cars. Sometimes I did it right, but the boss smiled the whole time. He signaled to his wife that everything was okay.

I lost track of time. I was overwhelmed by the lights, hunger, noise, and hard physical work that was required. The next thing I remembered was the boss tapping me on the shoulder.

"Alex, put the hoods over the cars while I close up. My wife is cooking something. We'll be done in fifteen minutes."

Boy, that was a long fifteen minutes. I could barely hang on. All the cars were lined up and had their hoods on.

"By the way, my name is Harold. Let's go inside. I'll introduce you to my wife, Jane."

I followed Harold inside the trailer. I observed it was spacious and decorated with taste. Harold went over and put his arm around his wife's waist, "Jane, meet Alex."

"Nice to meet you, Alex. You look pretty worn out. Have a seat," she said smiling.

"Hi, Jane. Do you mind if I freshen up a bit?" I asked.

"Great idea," said Jane, "since it's going to be another forty-five minutes before supper is ready. Harold, go into the closet. There are clean clothes in there that will fit Alex."

"Which closet?" Harold questioned.

"You know, the one where you store your tool box."

Harold preceded to show me the spare bedroom with a double

bed in it. It was more comfort than I had experienced in two years.

"Shower next door," as he pulled out a shirt and some pants out of the closet.

He'd barely stepped out the door before I was stripping off my clothes. There was a towel he must have laid out when I wasn't looking. I grabbed it and stepped out in the hallway. Jane was making noise with her pots and pans, and Harold was channel surfing with the remote control while sipping a cold beer.

I pulled the bathroom door closed behind me. *Were these people for real?* I thought. There had been no questions about my appearance, and unless they had major sinus problems they had to have noticed my smell. Here I was in their home. *There are still decent, caring people in the world*, was my realization as I turned on the water and soaked my body in the soothing warm water. I soaped myself and rinsed off, wanting to laugh and cry at the same time. What a joy! A hot shower has to be one of the greatest pleasures in life. I stayed a long time, but running out of hot water made me jump out and shave quickly.

I dried my hair, and even slapped on a bit of aftershave. I went into my room and put on the clothes Harold had laid out for me. It was time for some serious business — food.

As I came out of the bedroom, Jane and Harold looked at my transformation in disbelief, and then laughed. Harold turned off the TV immediately.

Jane greeted me, "Come on, Alex, have a seat any place at the table."

"No, right here at the head of the table. You did a great job today," said Harold.

"Yes, you did," echoed Jane. "Without you we would've had to close early. With no training you sure put on a show."

"Yeah, and the way you looked, I didn't think you'd last twenty minutes out there," Harold laughed.

"What do you want to drink?" asked Jane.

"Something fizzy," was all that I could utter overcome by her genuine kindness, although still a little suspicious.

She reached into the freezer and pulled out a few ice cubes. She put them in a glass and got a soda out of the fridge as I sat down at the head of the table. My emotions were overwhelming me. I couldn't remember the last time I had sat in a home for a meal.

"So tell me, Alex, where are you from?" asked Harold.

"Here, there, everywhere," I replied, uneasy about answering questions.

Harold just took a long sip of his beer. "Okay. If you don't want to tell me, fine. I was just trying to make conversation."

"No, it's not that, I'm just..."

"It's all right. I'm glad we found you, or you found us. Here, have some soup," Harold said.

"Vegetable beef, homemade," said Jane.

"Have some bread with it," as Harold passed me a basket full of rolls.

I was in such a rush, I burned the roof of my mouth with the first sip of the soup and had to quickly take a swallow of soda to ease the pain. Unable to remember when I had eaten last, my stomach reminded me to go slowly. So I sipped the broth and added small bites of bread between each spoonful of soup. Later, Jane brought out a pot roast with potatoes, carrots, and plenty of gravy. I felt like I was on top of the world.

"It's wonderful," I said, breaking the silence.

"We're glad you like it," said Harold. "By the way, today is Sunday, and tomorrow we're closed. That means I don't work, which is just as well, because you are going to be sore tomorrow."

"You think so?"

He kinda cocked his head, "After the physical labor you did today, I'd bet on it."

"I didn't think of it that way. It's been so long since the day of the week mattered," I verbalized.

"Well, you just sleep in. Harold will be outside, and I'll be cleaning the house," Jane announced as she started to clean off the table.

"What time is it now?" I wondered out loud.

"One AM," they said in unison.

"You didn't eat much. Nothing was wrong, I hope," said Jane.

"No. I'm just not used to such a feast and eating that much, but it was great."

She seemed to accept my response not knowing how I had understated my eating habits and asked, "Want some desert?"

"Could I save it for tomorrow?" Realizing that she might need some help, I took my plate to the sink.

"Sure. The fridge is right here if you get hungry in the middle of the night," she mentioned.

Rubbing my stomach, "Me? I don't think so."

"Well, Harold does it all the time."

"Jane!" Harold tried to look shocked, but couldn't contain his laughter.

"What? Did you think that I didn't know?"

"All right, you caught me. I think I'll go and read my newspaper," winking at me as he got up and headed for his recliner.

"You do that." She touched his hand gently as he walked by her.

Jane turned around to talk to me. "Go to bed when you are ready. I'll have some food prepared for you in the morning. We don't get up before noon."

"Mighty nice of you. I'm sure I won't either," I said. "Good night, and thanks for everything."

"You too," said Harold as I passed him on my way to my room. He was already engrossed in an article.

I went into my room, took off my clothes, and slid between the fresh linen sheets. I pulled the covers over my head, and the next thing I knew sunshine was bathing my whole room. The sun was high in the sky. It took me a moment to remember where I was.

I had had no dreams, no voices, no confusing feelings. So many good things had happened in the last twenty-four hours. *It must be a dream*, I thought to myself.

That first movement caused me to moan.

Oh, yeah, the bumper cars. My muscles were jumping and screaming in agony. This was definitely no dream.

Very slowly I extracted myself out of the bed. I wrapped a towel around my waist and headed into the bathroom for a shower. The hot shower brought me back. I dried my body and brushed my teeth with a toothbrush Jane had left for me. I went back to the room and put on the new clothes. Then I walked into the living room. The trailer was deserted. The TV was off, and there was a light in the kitchen with a note on the table.

"Help yourself," was all it said.

I decided to step out and smell the fresh air. I opened the door, and Jane was sitting just outside the door on the step knitting a sweater.

"For my husband," she said. "Do you want me to fix you something to eat?"

"Not right now, thank you."

"How about some coffee?"

"Yeah, that sounds great. Where is Harold?" I asked.

She laid the knitting down, "I'll go make some. Harold would probably like some too. He's greasing the wheels. He does it every week."

"Maybe I can help him," I said as I started toward the cars.

She called to me, "Tell him I'll bring him coffee."

"Yes, ma'am."

"Alex, you don't want to make me feel old, do you. Call me Jane, please."

I turned and saluted, "Jane it is."

Harold was sitting on the floor with grease up to his elbows.

"Can I help?" as I stooped down balancing myself with the steel bar feeling the muscles in my legs tighten with pain.

"No. Just ten more minutes and I'll be done. This is my last car. I've been at it for the past two hours." Harold added, "How'd you sleep?"

"Best night's sleep I've had in a long time. Jane is bringing us some coffee."

Harold put the wheel back on. He tightened up the nut bolts and dropped the jack. "Great. Just in time to wrap up and wash my hands."

He wiped his hands on a towel before grabbing his tools and the pail of grease. "How are the muscles, Alex?"

"Excruciating," I admitted.

"Told you," he smiled.

"I'm glad we're off today."

We walked to the shed, and I opened the door while he put the tools in their right places. Jane appeared with two cups of steaming coffee. She had brought a tray with cookies, cream, and sugar.

"I forgot the spoon. Harold takes it black. I didn't know how you liked it."

"No need, Jane, I just take cream." We all sat down and chatted.

The whole week went by so fast. The soreness in my body got

better every day. I slept without dreaming. My appetite returned. I could eat two meals a day plus a snack from time to time. As expected, I got better and faster at jumping the cars, and now Jane and Harold treated me like a son.

After a week my stomach had expanded again, and Harold called me the "vacuum cleaner with teeth". They put their belief and trust in me. It had been such a long time since that had happened to me, and I was grateful for it.

I was constantly smiling. We got up every morning around eleven AM and drank coffee. Harold took this time to tell me his story. He told me where he stopped to put up his ride, where and how he met Jane, how long he'd been doing this job. The ride was a legacy from his father.

I appreciated his honesty and willingness to tell me his story, but I wasn't quite ready to tell mine. I was blocking the past for now, what little of it I remembered. I needed more time before I could even think about all that had happened. He knew I was a kid from the streets, but he was smart and respectful and didn't ask questions.

Jane was always cooking or washing dishes, straightening the trailer, always busy. That was the most discreet woman I had ever met. There was definitely a feeling of trust growing in me.

"Harold," I said one Sunday.

"Yes, Alex?"

Before I realized it, I was pouring out my story to him. I was really relieved to have someone to talk to and surprised at how much I remembered. Maybe Jack's death had shook something loose. I told him all that I could remember about Mom, Dad, Adam, the shadow, and the void. Then I really got wound up telling him about the street kids, especially Simon, One Eye, and Jack, and how we pulled together. It took me close to three mornings to tell him, and he never interrupted. Every morning I picked up where I had left off the day before, and he would sip his coffee and listen.

In the afternoon, we would run the ride for the kids. It was truly another good week. No worries about anything, just working and living in the moment. During the second week I started to think about the other kids, but I needed more time to regain my energy.

The following weeks were spent getting to know all the folks operating the other rides. When I had some slack time, I walked around and everyone got to know me. "Alex, come get some roasted peanuts," or "Come have some cotton candy." Sometimes it was, "Come play the water pistol race, it's on me." I was the new kid there and became a new member of the family. It was truly a fairy tale life.

Every night when I returned to my room after a shower and watching TV and talking to Harold, I took the time to savor my good fortune. I felt safe in this room. The peace it emanated was enough to bring back a feeling I hadn't felt in a long time. Hope.

Every Sunday night like clockwork, Harold brought me my pay and said, "Thank you." It was me who should've been thanking him, but he genuinely felt good about my being in his home. Jane, on the other hand, had observed that I had a voracious appetite for chocolate brownies. She made sure we never ran out of them. The whole five weeks we had brownies. A couple of nights I wept tears of joy and appreciation in my bed overwhelmed by their kindness and charity.

During the third week, Sam came back, still in the cast for his broken leg. He had gone to visit some of his family and had come by to visit his old boss. He stayed for the day, then left.

The last days sneaked up on us faster than anyone expected. Harold, Jane, and I were all silent as we sipped our coffee. We all knew what was coming. Funny how you can get attached to someone so quickly. We spent the whole day disassembling equipment. We pulled the steel bars out of the ground and unbolted the steel panels from the floor. Next, we piled the panels onto the truck, followed by the cars on a trailer. The overhang mesh we rolled up, and coiled up all the electric cords. Everyone associated with the carnival was breaking down their rides. The day went by so fast with little time for talk.

By evening, everything was on the truck and trailer. Harold made one last tour to see if anything was missing. Then we all went inside for supper. Jane prepared my favorite meal, beef noodle soup, chicken in brown gravy, rice, sweet peas, and of course, brownies. *Who knows when I would eat like this again*, I thought.

During dinner we chatted about everything irrelevant. We were all too sad to look at each other in the eye. Harold got up and came back with an envelope that he presented to me.

I opened it up in silence. There was a note of thanks and five hundred dollars. "What's this for?"

"The $225 is for your last pay with an additional $275 as a bonus for a job well done."

"But..."

"Not a word," said Harold, "A simple thank you will suffice."

Words failed me. I just nodded.

"Our address is in there. If you come down south, you always have a room and friends who will be glad to see you."

"And brownies," added Jane.

"We come here every year, at this time," continued Harold, "So come out to see us."

"You two are the best."

"There is also the name of a lumberyard. I have a distant cousin that I see every year when I am in town. Go to see him, and say hello for me. I'm pretty sure he will have work for you."

I knew exactly where the yard was located, and I felt proud that Harold would recommend me. "I'll go Thursday."

"Good, 'cause you're starting Monday."

Standing in disbelief I stammered, "You mean I have a job already?"

Harold had all the details, "Yes, it's all arranged. You'll be in training for a few weeks learning the layout, doing some stocking at night. I told him what a hard worker you are."

"I don't know what to say, I'm truly touched."

"Say nothing, just go and he'll explain the whole job to you. I don't know what the pay will be, but he's fair."

"If he's as fair as you are, I'll be rich in three months."

Jane and Harold laughed. We were eating our brownies and enjoying the moment. After dinner, we went to the local diner to celebrate.

"My treat," I said, but they would have nothing to do with it. Harold picked up the tab.

Back at the trailer, I was in my room when I realized that this was the last time I was going to sleep here. On the bed were the clothes I had worn when I arrived, all washed, ironed, and folded in an opened suitcase. I went out and found Jane in the recliner.

"Harold's in the shower," Jane said.

"You know why I came out."

"Look, the suitcase is for you. Also the clothes you wore while working for us. Just take it, it's the least we can do." I knew it wasn't a request, but an order. I walked over and said, "Thanks." Then I leaned over and gave her a kiss on the cheek and turned around and went into my room. There was nothing more to say.

Nine AM. The smell of coffee brewing woke me. I put on some shorts and a t-shirt and wandered out into the living room. Jane was walking around the trailer.

"So you slept well," she said laughing.

"What's so funny?"

"Your hair is all which a ways."

"Oh, yeah, it does that," I said combing my fingers through my hair.

"That's better," she said. "Come and get your coffee. Want some toast?"

"Yes, thanks. Where's Harold?"

"Talking with the other owners. We're all leaving at eleven AM."

For just a second I wished I was going with them, "Where to exactly?"

"We all put our money together and bought land in Louisiana. We leave the equipment there during the winter months."

Harold came in around ten AM. "All the guys are ready," he said, "We'll be pulling out on time."

I went around one more time, shaking hands with everyone and gave a few hugs, especially to the girls close to my age.

At eleven AM I gave Jane a real big hug. She had tears in her eyes. I shook hands with Harold. It was short and sweet. Harold helped Jane into the truck and went around the front and got into the cab. He started the engine, put it into first gear, and the truck moved forward. He didn't look back.

It was better that way. I was standing in the middle of the fairgrounds holding my suitcase. Paper littered the place, and the place felt empty after all the activity from the past five weeks. I had just experienced living with decent, caring human beings.

I took the first bus going to the center of town. Wow, what an ordeal! I had never ridden a bus before, and I didn't realize that "exact change" meant "exact change". I had to ask three people before I had exact change and could finally get on the bus. The driver had the personality of a barn door. I sat three rows behind him, and asked, "Is it extra to sit down?" He just rolled his eyes and kept driving.

We passed many gray buildings, company trucks, tractor trailers, and parking lots filled with cars. I noticed a few small factories and oilfield equipment piled up behind chain-link fences. This part of town had no character whatsoever, strictly industrial.

Slowly trees started to appear, along with nice suburbia houses with manicured lawns. Some had white picket fences, dogs, and all the extras. Then the traffic became heavy, and the bus got crowded. I gave up my seat to let a pregnant woman sit down. She smiled in thanks and seemed surprised by my courtesy.

I looked at all the people on the bus. There were all types, all ages, and races from different walks of life. Most were dosing off or daydreaming, but they all had a look of hopelessness on their faces. I got a cold chill down my back.

The feeling was too scary. I decided right then and there that I was going to get off of the streets for good and do something with my life.

Jane, Harold, and everybody at the fairgrounds were always

smiling, singing, laughing, helping each other or just visiting. I had experienced the way that I wanted to live — like they did, with a happiness that was contagious. I had spent five weeks in a place where no questions were asked. You were accepted just as you were and genuinely welcomed.

I suddenly realized that we were downtown. I got off the bus and looked for the connection to my part of town — slum city. I found it and gave the bus driver my transfer ticket. He was much nicer than the first driver. The bus was almost empty. I went to the back of the bus and sat down.

I started to think about my future. I had worked for five weeks. No one had let me pay for anything, and room and board had been included. Harold had given me an extra week's pay. Thus far, I had spent only ten dollars. I had $1,350 plus a job waiting on me. My goal was clear. I am going to get an apartment and start over.

Lips was the first one to see me when I walked into the abandoned building. "Alex, where have you been? We've been worried."

"Working," was all I said.

The rest of them jumped up and crowded around me. I had questions coming at me from everyone including two kids I'd never seen before.

"Whoa, whoa. Hold on guys. Let me walk in first," as I put my bag down.

"We had everyone on the street looking for you," Lips ignored me and kept talking as usual.

"Yeah," said One Eye.

I looked around. Nothing had changed.

"All right, sit down, and be quiet. What have you guys been up to?"

"You first," they all insisted.

"Well, what's with Butterball?" seeing him stretched out on the floor.

"I'm sick, Alex," he moaned.

"I'll take care of you. Now, everyone sit down and I'll tell you what happened."

I spent the next three hours telling them about my five weeks. They were hanging on my every word. I talked about the fair, the lights, Jane and her brownies. I told them how I would jump from bumper car to bumper car collecting the tickets. I talked about my warm bed, the fattening food, greasing the wheels each week, and the daily showers. I described Harold and his jovial outlook on life. I mentioned the fresh laundry, and the smiling crowds. I talked with so much passion, even Lips stayed quiet the whole time. Nobody noticed that it was dark by the time I finished.

We all went to see Maggie at the donut shop for a celebration.

"Hi, Maggie."

"Hey, Alex, where have you been? Everyone's been looking for you, even Rick."

"You don't say. Just got a job," I said casually.

She had her hands on her hips, "Peggy was worried sick, since you never went to the shelter for food or a shower."

"You see, I'm doing all right. Even put on some weight," motioning to my waist.

"I must say, you're looking good," she said and added softly, "By the way, I was so sorry to hear about Jack."

"Thanks, Maggie." Before I could say more, several people had come over to ask questions about "the job." The curiosity and excitement was skyrocketing with everyone talking at once. I calmly assured them that I would give them all the details later.

Maggie stood there patiently waiting to take our order.

"Five cups of coffee, and two lemonades, and the bill is on me," I finally got to reply.

"Coming up." She was back in no time with drinks and some donuts.

"The donuts are on me," she added with a smile.

After we devoured the donuts, I turned and asked, "All right, Lips, who are these kids?"

"The chubby one on your right is Andre. The other one with freckles is Ellis," he answered. "They were huddled together near our building about a week ago, and we kinda became big brothers to them."

I couldn't help but notice how young they were and remember how bad it had been for me at first.

Lips continued, "We've fed them and given them a safe place to sleep and kept the druggies and perverts away from them."

"Good enough." I excused Lips and myself from the group and found us another table. "Now tell me about Jack."

"Everything we know is sketchy," Lips muttered without

looking me in the eyes.

Putting the cup down on the table I faced him and placed my hand on his, "I don't care, Lips, you were there with him that night, so don't beat around the bush. Tell me everything you remember."

"Well, we were walking around,"

"No bull, Lips, it's me, Alex, you're talking to."

"As I said, we were walking when Jack spotted a man getting out of his car to go in a package store. You know, the one where Martin works."

"Yeah, yeah, go on," I pushed.

He took a sip of coffee and continued, "Jack saw an opportunity and said 'See you at home' as he went toward the idling car. The owner of the car wasn't even inside the store when he happened to look back and saw Jack moving towards his car. He spun on his heels and with a running leap, jumped on Jack grabbing him by his jacket. Jack slid out of the jacket and took off like a rocket."

"Where was Simon all this time?" I interrupted again with a purpose.

"Let me see. Oh, yeah, the Ghost was just pulling into the parking lot."

What a coincidence, I thought to myself. "Then what?" I asked.

"Well, that's all. Jack ran like mad, the guy chased him for a hundred yards and gave up. He threw Jack's jacket and cursed at the night. He came back, turned off his engine and went inside."

"And?"

"Ghost and I went into the night to search for Jack and found him behind the bakery, flat on his back." He stopped and just stared at the cup. "He must have tried to go up the fire escape, but some of the bolts were rusty and I guess they broke under his weight and he fell back with the metal ladder on top of him."

"Anything else?"

"No," was all he said. Lips was swallowing hard and fighting back tears.

"What was Simon doing?" I hated to push, but for some reason I really needed to know.

"Nothing. He helped me pull the fire escape off Jack."

"That's it?" thinking to myself that there had to be more. *Was it just a freak accident?*

"Ghost looked at him and said 'I think he's dead, go get the others.' Next thing I know you were shaking me like a prune tree."

We sat there for a few more minutes and then returned to the group, and I told everyone, "I want all of you to stay away from Simon."

"Why do you want us to stay away from Simon?" asked Lips.

"He gives me the creeps, that's all. Just a premonition. Trust me."

I was silent for awhile, trying to put my thoughts in order before I spoke again. "I can't figure him out. He only appears at night, he pushes us to steal for him, and we don't know anything about him. He's evil, I'm telling you."

"Alex, don't spook me. I already feel like hell," Butterball moaned.

I smiled back at Butterball and said, "Well, guys, you won't be living at the 'Ritz' much longer."

"What are you talking about?" they asked almost in unison.

"You'll see."

I needed to talk to Maggie, so I got her attention. After attending three tables she came over.

"Yes, Alex?"

"Listen. What are you doing tomorrow?"

"Why? You want a date?" she asked, leaning toward me.

Catching me a little off guard, I gulped, "Tempting, but for now, I need your help."

"Name it," was her reply.

"I need your shower. I have a job interview tomorrow."

"Way to go," she answered with a thumb's up motion.

"I also need you to go with me to the office at your apartment complex to vouch for me. I'm going to get an apartment, two bedrooms if they have one," I added.

At that moment Maggie's mouth fell open along with everyone else's.

"Stop staring, Maggie, I know I'm not that good looking."

"Yes you are," she replied, "but don't let it go to your head."

"Ooh, that's a come on if I ever heard one," said One Eye, smiling and jabbing me in the ribs.

"Knock it off," I said blushing.

"Red becomes you," said Lips.

"Can't take the heat, pretty boy?" Butterball perked up to harass me.

"Help me out, Maggie."

"Keep me out of this. You can handle it."

She smiled and turned to check on the other tables. We all hung around for a while longer with each one taking a turn at telling me what they had been doing while I was gone. There was a really festive, family feeling to our group. I asked One Eye, "What do you know about the brothers?"

"Well, they're not really brothers. Like I said, they were together when we found them, so we called them the brothers. Besides, they go everywhere together. Both of them were bruised pretty badly. Dirty, hungry, and we couldn't get them to tell us anything."

The two brothers were happily sitting in a booth, munching on another order of donuts. Each had sugar from the donuts on their faces. I handed the "brothers" some napkins and tried to get a little more information, "Hey, brothers, what are your names again?"

"I'm Andre."

"I'm Ellis," said the freckled one.

"How old are you?"

"I'm nine," said Andre with pride.

"I'm ten, and I can count to one hundred," Ellis boasted.

"That's great. I need to talk to Butterball for a moment. I'll be right back."

Butterball and I moved to another booth. Maggie came over

with refills and sat down for a few minutes. I told her about the job I had. She was so happy for me. A couple of customers came in, and she hopped up and went back to the grindstone.

Butterball was fading fast. He was white as a sheet. "Listen, Alex, are you really getting an apartment?"

"That's what I want to talk to you about. I'm going to get a two bedroom. I have the down payment, and I want to share it with you, Bill, Lips, and One Eye."

"Bill hasn't been around for the last ten days," he said.

"He'll come back." I knew instinctively.

"Why me, Alex?" Butterball seemed like a little kid asking this question.

"If you need to know, Jack asked me to take care of you, and to make sure nothing happens to you." It just came to me, and they couldn't argue with my reasoning. "Now stop asking so many questions, and let's go."

"When are we moving in?" grinning with pleasure, Butterball seemed to feel better immediately.

"I'm going to look tomorrow, but it may take about a week or so. Now let's go." Getting up to leave and walking over to the register, I waited to complete the plans with Maggie for tomorrow.

She told me that she was off the next day, and I arranged to meet her at her apartment about noon so she could take me to the office.

Since Lips had taken the kids home, Butterball and I walked back in silence to our hideaway. The streets were deserted. When we arrived everyone was still talking, except for the brothers, who were fast asleep. They slept in the corner clutching each other.

"Well, I'm going out for a stroll," realizing that I needed to walk and sort out my plans.

"Need some company?" asked Lips.

"If you want to go that's fine, but I'm not much for talking."

"That's okay, it's just good to have you back."

Butterball was already laying down. Lips grabbed the extra blanket and draped it over him and said, "I won't need it."

We left the building quietly and walked along the streets of this miserable neighborhood in silence. We had followed this same route a thousand times, and I never got used to it. The absurdity of life on the street was getting to me. Harold had made me realize that there was so much more to living. The brownies helped, of course. Man, they were good. Well, tomorrow I'm getting an apartment. That's a first step.

Lips snapped me out of my thoughtful state, "Hey, look, Alex. There's Rick."

"Hey Rick, do any heroic acts lately?" I called him over to us. Rick was like everyone else anxious to hear my story, so we walked to the park.

"You've put on the bacon," he observed checking me out.

"Three meals a day did it to me," I enjoyed telling him about the fair, brownies, and the good life.

He sniffed in my direction, "Jeez, you even smell good."

After listening patiently, Lips said, "By the way, Rick, we got two kids in our building. We call them the brothers. They're really young."

"Say no more, I'll come pick them up tomorrow."

"Where are you taking them?" I asked.

"Peggy told me the city started a program for kids under twelve."

Lips and I both felt relieved and told him so with a high five.

"I'll get by your place first thing in the morning," he added with authority.

We spent the whole night talking. I told Rick what had happened, and then about my plans for the future. Lips never said a word for several hours. He was all ears for a change.

"Sounds great. Maybe I could get a job," said Rick.

"But how can we? It's impossible to find a regular shower, hard to sleep, and we're always worrying about food," Lips jumped in with Rick shaking his head in agreement.

"I know, I know. But after I get an apartment, you know that you can come shower every day."

"Hey, that would be a good beginning." Rick was smart and had come a long way.

"Well, it's getting light, and I've got to get some sleep before I go over to Maggie's."

He looked at me like he wanted to ask a question, but instead just said, "Don't forget, I'm coming to get the brothers."

"Okay. Tell Peggy I'll see her soon."

We walked back to our place. Lips was so tired he almost fell on his face and was snoring immediately. I wished I had it so easy. Usually I spent a fair amount of time chasing my demons. Besides, I had to go see Maggie in a couple of hours. It would be good to doze for a few hours.

I was half asleep when Rick came to pick up the brothers after a few hours. They were very quiet. So I rolled over and buried myself in my blanket.

When I woke up, the sun was high in the sky. Shoot, I was already late getting to Maggie's. I jumped up and ran all the way to her apartment. I was out of breath when I knocked on the door and smiled sheepishly as she opened it.

"It's 1:15, where were you?" With both hands on her hips, she stood blocking the doorway.

"Give me a break. I don't have a watch." I could tell she wasn't really mad but just giving me a hard time.

"You're going to need one if you are going to work," she was still blocking the door.

"I'll find one," I shuffled my feet noticing my sweat soaked shirt.

"I have one, and you can borrow it for now. Let's go."

"Hey, can't I wash my face? I just ran ten blocks, and I look like hell."

"Come on in. I'll show you where everything is."

"Nice place." I looked around as she pulled out some towels and found me a clean t-shirt.

After freshening up she locked the door behind her, and we walked over to the office. In no time everything was taken care of since Maggie did most of the talking. She told them I was from out of town, and she would vouch for me. Her recommendation went a long way and made everything go smoothly. I would have to wait a couple of days while they cleaned an apartment that had been recently vacated.

Afterward Maggie drove me to the lumberyard, where according to Harold, there was supposedly a job waiting for me. We arrived around three PM. She parked the car, and we walked over to the customer service counter.

"Hi, I came to speak to Big Joe."

"No one here by that name," said the girl at the counter.

Bummer, there goes my luck, I thought to myself. A tiny five-foot tall guy turned around, and looked at me, "Alex?"

"You bet."

"Harold phoned me. When can you start?"

It was that simple. I had the job based solely on Harold's recommendation. After telling him that I could start right then and there, he told me that the next day would be fine.

I introduced Maggie to Joe, and we talked a little about Jane. Then he told me that jeans and a t-shirt were satisfactory work clothes. I was still having trouble believing my good fortune when I heard my new boss say, "Then I'll see you tomorrow at 5:30 PM. Oh, by the way, only Harold calls me Big Joe."

"Whatever you say boss. I'll be here."

"Nice meeting you, miss," he said to Maggie.

We walked out to the car. I was still stunned. Just a handshake, and I had a job. Harold really knew how to take care of things. We had barely reached the car when Joe ran up to us, "Hey, Alex."

I turned around surprised. "Listen, we're short-handed around here. You know anybody willing to work?"

"Yes, I know someone."

"Bring him with you tomorrow. Same as you, in jeans and a t-shirt at 5:30 PM. I'll explain the job tomorrow." He was already stepping on a fork lift shuffling a pile of wood.

"Congratulations!" Maggie spoke for the first time, "Where to now?"

"Nothing to do until tomorrow night. Let's go to the park downtown, the one by City Hall," I suggested.

She drove through the maze of streets. The closer we got to downtown the more traffic we had to deal with. People were rushing everywhere like a bunch of ants. I was so overwhelmed. New job. A place to live. Riding in a car. Chatting about sweet nothings with a girl. It was all happening too quick for me. *Just take a deep breath and go with the flow*, I told myself.

"What are you thinking about, Alex?"

"Oh, nothing in particular, except things are happening so fast."

"Don't chicken out," she teased me.

"Who me? I just held a job for five weeks. I didn't know anything when I started, and I ended up doing a great job. Besides, I like what is happening to me and I've decided I'm not going back."

"That's the spirit, Alex. Here's the park. Help me look for a parking space."

We parked and locked her car. We had been walking in the park for a few minutes when I spied an ice cream stand. I bought us two ice cream cones. I don't think I had eaten ice cream since I left home. It felt good licking on that cold cone while strolling down the path. Maggie grabbed my hand. It startled me. "Maggie, why are you holding my hand?"

She shook her head tossing her hair in the wind, "It feels good. Why else?"

It did feel good but a little uncomfortable at the same time, "Well, you're really nice and pretty, but things are moving too quickly. I need some time to absorb all of this."

"I'm just holding your hand."

"Yes, but understand for the time being, I can't get involved. I've got too many things to take care of."

"I never said, 'Let's get involved.' I was just holding your hand," she said and pulled her hand away.

"I know, I'm overreacting, but I have personal stuff going on."

She casually commented that she had heard about my shadow and nightmares that caused me to scream out in my sleep.

"Sounds like everybody on the street knows. I might as well write to the local paper and tell the whole city, but you must see how important it is for me to settle this part of my life," hoping she would just let this conversation end.

"Yes, I do," taking my hand again. "By the way, I saw Simon after you left last night."

"What did he want anyway? He's a creep, and I don't trust him."

"Just to say Hi, and asked how you were dealing with Jack's death."

"I haven't seen him since he held Jack in his arms, and I don't care if I ever see him again. Please don't tell him anything about me. For now, let's just enjoy the park. I don't want to think about it anymore."

We walked in silence very conscious of each other's presence, acknowledging our pleasure with an occasional exchange of smiles. She was generous, as usual, when she broke the silence with, "By the way, if you would like, feel free to come by my apartment and shower before you go to work."

"Can I bring Tony, I mean One Eye, so he can clean up too?"

"Of course. He's welcome, too," she answered.

"What time should we come over?"

"When we get home, I'll give you the extra key."

"Thanks."

We walked slowly while we finished our ice cream. It didn't bother me that she was holding my hand. I had been clear, and I felt better about it. We sat on a bench and talked about lots of unimportant things, just getting to know each other. When Maggie got tired, we drove back to our part of town, and I kissed her before leaving her at her door. It was very special.

"Night, Maggie."

"Goodnight, Alex. See you later."

I went back to the shelter. I needed to tell One Eye about his coming to work with me at the lumberyard.

He was sitting in the middle of the room eating a sandwich when I walked in. Butterball was curled up in the corner. I asked him if he felt any better and if he had eaten. He told me One Eye had already taken care of him. Friends are like that. I told One Eye about the job, and he was excited. I was so tired at that point, I stretched out and went to sleep.

◇ ◇ ◇ ◇ ◇

The sun was high in the sky when I woke up. One Eye was ready to go, "Alex, glad you're up."

"Morning to you too. Let's go to the shelter and see Peggy and get some food." The word food always got One Eye's attention.

Peggy was extremely glad to see me. She understood how hard Jack's death had hit me and was glad that I was back. She looked great and was always as pleasant as she was supportive to all of us. "Rick told me you have a job and are getting an apartment. Alex, I'm really happy for you," she said, "How about something to eat to celebrate your job?"

"Twist my arm, Peggy," I answered.

"Hey, Tony, feeling good today?"

"Real good, Peggy."

She never called us by our nicknames, it seemed to be her way of showing respect. She always had a kind word for everyone, never gave advice and never judged. Oh, she had her problems, too. She kept the shelter open late always giving more than she was paid for, and made time to listen to all the hurt. On top of that, the city gave her hell for bending the rules and threatened to replace her. She would just shrug her shoulders and sigh in resignation. She was a real gem.

After a good meal that restored our strength, One Eye and I went to see Joe. We even arrived a little early. Joe was surprised.

"No one gets to work early."

"Hi, Joe. We're just eager to start."

"Who is your friend?"

"Tony, but we call him One Eye."

"Well, not at work you don't. Here we respect each other and what would the customers think if I have Sam saying over the PA, 'One Eye, customer assistance in aisle fifteen.' No way am I getting into this one."

"Got you, Joe. Tony it is."

Tony and I went to the office to fill out some paperwork, and became familiar with the place. We were assigned to a fellow named Karl. We followed his every move to learn the tricks of the trade. It didn't take long to learn how to smile and be pleasant to the customers and restock the shelves. After a week we were answering questions and were able to find just about everything. We still had a lot to learn, but we were free from following Karl around all the time.

Karl was a nice guy, but we didn't really relate to him, and he couldn't understand what we had been through. I wasn't about to explain. As for Tony, he still could not believe his good luck. He would follow me in the aisles, saying how it felt like he was living in a dream.

A few days after starting our jobs, we moved into the apartment with the Rick and Maggie's help. There was a lot of laughter and feelings of disbelief and joy. I was so glad we got an apartment on the far side of the complex. That way there were no complaints about the kids coming in and out taking showers, resting, and just hanging out, in a safe place. We had an electric stove, and everyone agreed that hot soup was definitely better than cold. Life was great.

One day at work I heard over the PA, "Alex Beard, please report to the office."

What do they want? I asked myself as I excused myself from a customer. I walked over to the office and went inside.

"Hi, Janet, what's going on?"

She was sitting at the front desk and answered without even looking up from her work, "Joe's waiting on you."

"Okay." I knocked on the door and waited until I heard him say to come in, and I went inside his office.

"Alex, have a seat."

I was always impressed with the neatness and cleanliness of Joe's office. "Hi, Boss. What can I do?"

"Listen, I was looking over your application. Are you related to the Beard of Beard and Knight Excavating and Foundations?"

"Yes, I am. He's my father."

He just sat there a second, then asked, "What are you doing

here?"

"Long story," was all I felt like answering.

"Well, I won't ask, but you know his truck shows up here from time to time."

"I can't stop him, it's a free country." My discomfort was obvious as I squirmed in the chair.

"I know, but his men have been looking for you," he added.

Trying to hide my surprise, I smarted off, "Yeah, and I believe in Cinderella."

"Don't get smart with me, young man, I don't deserve it," Joe fired back.

"Sorry, Joe. There's lots of bad feelings. I cut all ties with him."

"Like I said, it's none of my business, but he is still looking for you, and he's a big businessman now." Joe was telling me something I didn't know.

"I would appreciate it if you don't tell him or any of his men that I'm working here."

"Okay. Now do you want to work more hours?"

"Whatever you can give me, I'll take."

"What about night watchman? It's more hours," he offered.

Sounded perfect to me, "Hey, I don't sleep much at night. That would be great."

"Done. You can start next week, but first I need to find someone to replace you." Joe explained that he wanted someone to start as soon as possible so I could show them the ropes. It didn't take anytime for me to think of Rick, so I told Joe that I was pretty sure I could bring someone in the next day.

"By the way, your friend Tony is doing a great job. Thank you for bringing him here."

"Glad you like him."

"Now get back to work." Joe really cared about people for all his tough appearance.

I went back to my aisle. Great. I was promoted after two weeks. What more could I ask for? I needed to ask Rick if he wanted a job. I just assumed he would want the job, but I had better check with him after work. He was always hanging around Bobby's restaurant. I focused back on my work and the customers.

It was 10:30 when I left the lumberyard. I raced over to Bobby's, but I had just missed Rick.

"Martin, where's Rick?"

"He went to the donut shop to see Maggie." I took off and ran to the donut shop and on the way found him standing on the corner begging for money to eat.

"Hey, Rick, stop begging."

"You buying?"

"No, you are. You've got a job at the yard." I couldn't hold my excitement any longer.

When he realized that he would be working with Tony and me and really making money on a job for the first time in his life, he grabbed me and gave me a bear hug, swinging me around off the ground. Suddenly sensing that it might look like we were dancing, he jumped back and said, "Great, man, when do I start?"

"Tomorrow night. You sleep at my place tonight and then you can shower in the morning."

"Loan me five bucks, Alex. I'm buying."

"Good. Let's celebrate."

We went in and had a good time. Maggie finished at midnight and joined us until we left at two AM. We all piled up in Maggie's car and laughed all the way home.

The next few months were relatively quiet. The apartment was like a revolving door for anybody who needed help and would follow the rules. We never locked the front door. I had not seen the shadow since Jack's death. I would hear about Simon from time to time. He would ask about me, but I told everyone to keep mum.

By then I was working as the night watchman as well as closing. Tony and Rick were still working, which made it easier to pay the bills. I still had my nightmares and the void when I closed my eyes, but I had reached a point where I could ignore it for the most part.

One evening as I was starting my shift, an older guy walked up behind me and caught me totally off guard.

"Hi Alex, you doing all right?"

I turned and looked right at him, but I couldn't place him. He looked familiar, but I got no name, no memory, no nothing when I saw him.

"You don't remember me, do you?" he said, smiling through his grey beard.

"Can't say I do," I confessed.

"Pat. Patrick McGill. I work with your dad."

"Right. How is the wife?" I answered, faking it.

"What wife? I have no wife."

Oops! First mistake, "Sorry. I forgot."

So many things from the past erased. Sure I know my name and where I'm from, I even remember Adam and Dad and the pain that I would like to forget. It's all the details — the details that make the difference that make you whole. That was what was gone.

"Listen. Your dad has been looking for you. Why don't you give him a call?"

"I didn't know," which was the truth.

"Come on. He misses you. I'll come over, and we'll barbecue like the old days.

"Well, I'll think about it," was all I could say.

"Just call him. Now that your dad is alone, I spend a lot of time at his place." He paused and then reluctantly added, "So I see his loneliness."

"I'll give it some thought, about calling Dad, I mean," I said.

"You do that, Alex. Well, I got to get going. Take care."

"So long."

Now that he was gone, I relaxed a little. It didn't take long, however, before my mind started to ask questions. *Did he miss me? Can I forgive him? Do I want to go back? What is the big deal? Why bother?* So many questions made the work much more difficult. I couldn't concentrate with this new distraction, maybe I should go talk to him. I didn't know anymore.

Boy, did Pat confuse me. I didn't even remember him. My head felt like it was going to explode. I thought those events were behind me, but no, they were coming back with a vengeance.

I didn't even hear the customers questions. Sam came by to ask if everything was all right. I brushed him off and said "Don't ask." He knew me well enough to know I was not in a mood to be pushed for details. I was freaking out, plain and simple. What a lousy feeling. I don't even remember closing or watching the yard. All I remember is Joe arriving to open the gates.

"Alex, you look like hell."

"Sorry, Joe. Can I go home?"

"Yeah, see you tonight."

"Have a nice day," I muttered.

I walked home without paying attention. I couldn't have told you if the sun was shining. All I remember is trying to control the anxiety, without much success. I arrived at the apartment, took a shower, ate something, changed clothes, listened to people talking. It was so irrelevant.

"Hey, snap out of it." Rick was shaking my arm, and One Eye was behind him with a puzzled look on his face. "Alex, have you seen a ghost or what?"

"Why?" barely hearing his voice.

"'Cause you're as white as a sheet."

I shrugged, "Never mind."

"Never mind, my foot. It's been over two and a half years of you snapping in and out. Well, deal with it, man." Rick was serious.

"It's my problem."

"Yeah, and someday you're gonna explode," Rick pushed, "It's time."

"All right. I'm going to take some time off."

"Good. I'll take care of everything here while you're gone."

"Appreciate it, Rick."

"Don't mention it. By the way, Alex, if you need to be covered at the yard, I can arrange it with Joe. Now sit down and eat."

"Okay. But ya'll get off my back." They had gotten to me. It was time.

Rick, Tony, and I sat down and ate a couple of chili dogs. Afterwards I went into my room to think things through. Maybe I ought to go home and see my father, talk things over.

At one time, if I remember correctly, he was a natural healer. He always said that the power of the universe can be shaped or tamed at will, if your intention is pure. Maybe I should take the time on my next day off to go and see him. I could ask him about my nightmares, the shadow, and above all, my lack of feeling.

I tried to close my eyes and get some rest, but too many thoughts were spinning through my mind. It was late morning before I finally passed out.

Butterball came in to shake me at five PM. Just enough time to get a shower and get to my shift. The evening dragged by. I couldn't wait until the morning, my day off was coming up. Now that I had made the decision, everything else seemed to fall into place. I would go home and face Zach, and see what happened.

Seven AM. I couldn't wait to get up. The evening before I phoned Maggie at work and asked if I could borrow her car. She was more than happy to accommodate me, and all I had to do was come pick it up.

Allen came in to open up the yard. My anxiety grew, and I left like a bolt of lightning.

"Bye, Allen."

"Where's the fire?"

"I'll tell you in a few days."

"Slow down, kiddo."

I was already turning the corner on my way to Maggie's apartment. The morning was already warm. It was going to be a real scorcher. I got to Maggie's apartment in less than fifteen minutes. She was waiting for me. She still had on her morning coat and had breakfast cooked.

"Good morning, Alex."

"Hum, what's cooking?"

"Come in and see for yourself. For once," she said, "you're my guest, and I can take advantage of the time we have together."

I stepped into her place as she shut the door behind us, and I immediately caught a whiff of something good cooking.

"You can invite me over anytime. It sure smells good." I leaned over and kissed her cheek.

"Yes, but it's kinda tough with both of us working at night," she motioned for me to sit down at the table.

"But if you cook like this, I might be over more often."

It felt nice to be in a kitchen — it reminded me of Harold and Jane's. Maggie was stirring something on the stove, and I even liked that she asked for my help, "How about getting the apple juice out of the fridge. The glasses are over the sink on the left."

I grabbed two glasses and the juice as she finished setting up the table. Her place was so simple and neat, not like my place where all my destitute friends were constantly dropping in to sleep, shower, rest, grab a warm bite to eat and feel safe.

"Alex, are you listening? Bring the toast from the oven and turn it off, please."

"Turn what off?" realizing she meant the oven, "Right, sorry long shift."

We sat down and ate the egg and sausage casserole, toast, juice and coffee that she had prepared, and I was right — it tasted just as good as it smelled. When I told her so she blushed and surprised me by jumping up and coming over and playfully punching my arm making me laugh which only aggravated her more. As I grabbed her wrists to stop her she pulled away causing both of us to fall on the floor still laughing. Suddenly I looked into her eyes and felt this overwhelming urge to hold her in my arms. It was a completely new experience to feel the warmth of another human being. In an instant, I was holding her, kissing her and caressing her hair like a starving man given his first meal in days.

Coming to my senses, I pushed her away, "Oh Maggie, I'm so sorry."

"What for?" she answered gently, "I care for you, Alex."

"But I don't know what came over me," I lamented.

"Maybe you just let yourself feel."

I stood up still shaken by the intensity of the moment. "I think I had better go." She handed me the keys leaning over and kissing me on the cheek, "Have a good day," was all that she added.

As I stepped out into the sunlight and walked to the car, I had a special and beautiful feeling that we would be together forever.

I started the car and rolled out of the parking lot with caution. For some reason the day seemed brighter, maybe it was the closeness I had experienced with Maggie that gave me a new outlook on life, whatever the cause I was excited about going to see my father.

After nearly two hours in the main stream of traffic on the interstate, I turned south and headed out into the country via a scenic four-lane road. With my memory on hold, it would be a lot of fun to find my way home after so many years. I vaguely remembered the road and a few landmarks, but mostly I found myself driving through open fields with fences covered with honeysuckle. Nothing so far gave me a clue. Not long after turning right, the road narrowed to two lanes, and after a few miles I saw a small stone church on the left that registered in my memory. That triggered a feeling of anticipation — *not too far now* — one small town to go through.

I was really starting to have butterflies in my belly signalling a little anxiety, but now I was too close to turn back.

On the other side of the second town I could see a small lake and recognized immediately the location where the tragedy had happened. Caught up in my memories I drove right into town and pass the house without recognizing it. Well, so much for concentration. Turning the car around, I drove slowly, and there on my right I saw our house. The landscape had changed — the bushes and trees were much larger and several flower beds had been added.

After parking the car in the driveway I walked to the front door and rang the bell. My hand was actually shaking, and I suddenly realized how dry my throat was. *Why worry? After all, it's no big deal. It has been nearly three years, but after all, he is my dad.* When no one came to the door, I rang again, but still no answer. Might as well try the back door — still no answer, but the door was open.

Entering the house I was unexpectedly overwhelmed by emotion. It had been so long, but as I walked into the house I was unprepared for my response to the smells, the sight of the furniture still arranged exactly the same way as the day I left, an ashtray half full on the coffee table, the remote and magazine on the top of the television, books everywhere. Nothing had changed except for the missing laughter of my brother Adam and myself. Wandering through the house I decided for some reason to go downstairs to the basement while waiting for my father to return.

I opened the door, turned on the light and went down the stairs. Mostly boxes — so I started snooping around — mostly junk and records for Dad's business, tools, more boxes with china and crystal wrapped in newspaper, clothes, boots, toys, and old pictures — nothing had been thrown away. I sat there looking through pictures of us playing baseball, the company barbecues, the three of us in front of the old church, an old photograph of my mother — she was such a beautiful woman. More photographs of Adam and I in the pickup truck, playing on the swing and fishing on the pier, but none of these pictures made sense.

I saw myself in the pictures and recognized Dad, Adam and Mom, but could not remember how it felt to be a part of the activities. Even the toys didn't have any special meaning. *Well, guess I might as well wait upstairs.*

Reaching the top of the stairs I was conscious of the smell of the house and had a fleeting memory, but couldn't make heads or tail of it. As I walked through the living room one more time everything was familiar, but seemed too far away to trigger my feeble memory. I went into the kitchen — I think that we had a lady who worked for us three or four days a week, but for the life of me, I couldn't think of her name. I opened the fridge "let me see" I whispered to myself — a drumstick seemed inviting. So I grabbed it, took a bite and savored the flavor and taste slowly as I walked into the study. The rays from the sun were seeping through the sheers flooding the room with a soft light. Dad's desk was cluttered with papers — blueprints, bills, notes, a framed photograph of Mom and another of Dad, Adam and me holding a soccer ball. As I opened the drawers looking for anything that might help me put all of these clues in context with the last three years, I heard a car pulling into the driveway. Good, it must be Dad. Returning to the living room, I saw him coming through the side door. Since he was not expecting anyone, let alone his son, he was visibly startled by my presence.

"Alex?"

"Yes, Dad, I'm here."

He just stood there obviously too emotional to say a word or move, so I decided to go to him. My heart is pounding, what do you say after almost three years —

"Help me, Father, this is not easy."

As I crossed the room toward him, he started toward me with his arms open wide. "Welcome home, Son, let me look at you," as he stepped back looking me over.

I noticed that he looked older, "It feels strange to be home after all this time." When I left he had seemed so tall, and now we stood shoulder to shoulder.

"Well, Alex, it will take you a little time to adjust. Are you staying long?" he asked, and quickly added "You know you can stay here for as long as you want. This is your home."

"Not really. I work in the city, and I have an apartment. I just came here to try to straighten things out."

We spent most of the day just talking, catching up, but somehow I felt too ashamed to reveal the details of my time on the street. It was easier to talk about my working on the bumper cars, the lumberyard, but I kept even those details vague. He told me about going back to work after my departure to just fill his time, expanding the company.

"Let me ask you something, Dad. Why did you kick me out?"

He looked shocked, "Me, kick you out, never? You were wondering around all night, sleeping all day — typical teenager — if I questioned you or asked for your help, you just ignored me. No answer — no response."

"So I was a teenager. So what? That was your reason for dumping me?"

"Your not doing anything didn't bother me. It was the fits of rage, the outburst of anger without any provocation or reason that were hard to deal with."

"I was hurting."

"We were all hurting, Alex." The sadness of the memory was genuine as he turned his face away.

"Yes, but the void was driving me crazy." Good, I said it. "I had a void, and it is still there and increasing."

"What void?" he asked visibly concerned. "What are you talking about? You've got to describe this void!"

"The void, Dad, the void in my head, in my head destroying my memories and..."

"Slow down, take a deep breath... slowly, talk to me."

Taking a deep breath... slowly I told him all about the nightmares increasing the terror, the loss of feeling, memories vanishing every night while I slept, vanishing into the void never to come back. I told him about going through the pictures in the basement, and none of them making any sense.

"Are you telling me that you have no feeling whatsoever?"

I was pacing as I spoke, "Nothing, not love, tenderness, my body is always numb constantly asking myself why everything is so screwed up around me."

"From what you are describing, Alex, I believe I know what is happening. Sit down. Prepare yourself for what I am about to say."

"Tell me. I can take anything you have to say, anything to help me understand what is happening to me."

"Alex, I am afraid that someone has stolen your soul."

"That's crazy! What do you mean stolen my soul? That can't be possible."

"Yes, it is possible by a powerful energy force." Sadly he shook his head.

I was struck by fear, the blood was exploding in my temples, inexorably the reality still escaping me. I was trying to fight this terrifying thought that someone had the power to yank my soul without my knowing or suspecting.

"Who could have done this to me, Zach?" Shouting, not realizing that I had called my dad for the first time by his given name.

"I have no idea, but we will find out. There are people with this power but no one has the right to take someone's soul. It is sacred. When did it happen?"

"I don't know other than it started here in the middle of the night soon after Adam's death, when you had a gathering here at the house."

"I remember — I had some guests over to show them my appreciation after signing a big contract." Zach sat quietly, "Are you absolutely sure? Are you sure it was that night?"

"Yeah, it was the same night, and I've had the nightmares nearly every night since then."

Dad started writing down names, "All right, let's start from there. Who was here that night? There was Pat, my foreman, Mr. Belvoz, my client, Sam, his accountant, and there was another guy, he was a financial advisor for my client, what was his name...?"

"Never mind his name, who else"," I impatiently queried.

"Mr. and Mrs. Belvoz, their secretary, the treasurer of the company and his fiance, and the corporate attorney, Winston..."

"Maybe there's no connection." My hopes dropped.

"Perhaps you're right, it was a long shot. Wait John Lanquish was the tall man's name. I had never met him before that night," he was still trying to remember, rubbing his temples as he paced around the room.

"What tall man are you referring to?"

"Humm... the financial advisor. I remember he had a mole on his chin on the right side and strange eyes."

It hit me like a slap in the face. I ran to the front door and made it to the front porch before I vomited violently — the thought alone had just ripped me apart. It was "Ghost," that low-life had my soul! Zach had followed me and came up behind me with a towel in his hand.

"What is it, Alex, tell me," he pleaded.

Grabbing the towel out of his hand I wiped my face, tears streaming down my face, trembling like a leaf in a high wind, some saliva still running down my chin. After a few minutes I calmed down a little. "Simon, that man is Simon. John Lanquish is Simon."

"Do you know that man?"

"Of course, but why was he here?"

He told me that he was introduced as an advisor to Mr. Belvoz and wasn't on the guest list.

"This man is evil. Why didn't you stop him?"

"Son, you're not rational. How could I have known? I had no idea."

Looking straight at my Dad I suddenly knew, "I have to stop this evil man."

I could feel the rage mounting. My own father does not understand, he can not grasp the magnitude of the horrors I have gone through. My knuckles are white from clinching my fist, my jaw is sore from grinding my teeth, I am filled with anger and pain.

"Please, Alex, calm down."

"Calm down, how can you tell me to calm down? You have no idea what is like to lose all feeling, not only about the past, but to not be able to feel the sun on your skin, the rain on your face, love in you heart. I haven't felt anything but fear and pain, do you hear me, nothing I could hold on to in three years... just a void. I can't distinguish the seasons, I haven't heard a bird singing, I don't recall admiring the moon. I see people smiling and children laughing, and I don't understand; in fact, it actually irritates me. The nightmares occur night after night, relentlessly, causing me to toss and turn, asking the same question... Why, why, why?... like a broken record."

"Maybe I can help," Zach responded and tried to console me.

"Dad, you just don't understand what I have had to endure." I was screaming inside for feeling cheated... I had been robbed of three years of my life, three years gone forever, and no hope for the future.

"No, I can't, but... let me help." Dad gently guided me by the shoulders back to the living room, shut the front door, stopped in the kitchen to get some juice, grabbed a couple of pills and brought them back to me. "Alex, take these. We need to talk, these will help."

"What are these?"

"It will calm you down a little," his voice soothing me a little. "Stay a few days and rest."

"Thank you." I drank the juice to help me swallowed the tablets. "I can't. I've got to find him."

"No... not tonight, you don't. Why is it that you won't listen? You don't know what you are up against."

I jumped out of my chair, ran toward the front door, across the porch, got into Maggie's car, frantically turning on the ignition.

"Alex, don't go!" he shouted from the porch.

"I have to... you have never understood"

He said a few more words that I chose not to hear. I couldn't hear anything for the anger in my head. I threw the car in reverse, spinning the wheels without looking behind me, pulled out of the driveway almost hitting Zach's car... slammed the car into first gear and spun the wheels for at least a half block. I was blinded by the anger driving like a crazy man down the small country roads. The shadow appeared silently but bigger than it had ever been, appearing very agitated, moving erratically from one side of the back seat to the other.

"What are you doing here?" I screamed.

An eerie feeling ran down my back as it continued to dance around the car. It didn't seem threatening, and strangely I was getting accustom to this thing whatever it is. Besides nobody or nothing is going to dictate my life.

"Hey you, whatever you are, tell me what you are and what you want or just go away, scram, vanish, fade away, dissolve. You're a nuisance, get out of my life."

It swirled around for twenty to thirty seconds, and "poof" it was gone as quickly and silently as it had appeared.

I shivered and tried to brush the uneasy feeling away from me. "What is that and what does it want from me?" I said to myself, but now with it gone I concentrated on just getting back to the city more confused than ever. I had no idea what time it was vaguely remembering the sun having set on the horizon as I left the house.

Figuring Maggie would still be at work, I dropped the car in the parking lot at her apartment deciding to avoid a conversation with anyone until I had a chance to sort the events of the previous hours.

Getting out of the car without consciousness I started running as though my very life depended on it.

Glimmer Of Hope

François Sigrist

Part Two

A very powerful spasm almost yanked me out of the bathtub. Now I remembered what had happened. The realization of having been shortchanged by life itself released the anger again, and I had trouble remembering how or when I got into the bathtub. Looking at my wrinkled skin as I sat in the stone cold water, I surmised that I must have been there a long time and had gradually recalled the last three years. Now my direction was clear... I must find Simon.

Slowly extracting my numb, shriveled body out of the water, I grabbed a towel, superficially dried myself and opened the bathroom door. Everyone was there in the living room waiting. Butterball, Rick, One Eye, Lips, and a couple of other kids just stared at me as I emerged through the door.

Lips as usual spoke first, "What happened to you?"

"Yeah, are you okay?" Butterball jumped in.

Rick came to my rescue and restored order, "Come on, guys, law of the streets 'Never ask questions'."

"Thanks, Rick."

"Well, we were all worried."

They, in turn told me how I had arrived at the apartment, tearing off my shirt and staggering into the bathroom, slamming the door and emerging hours later.

"I am all right."

"If we can help, just ask." Lips and the rest of the gang gave me a sad smile.

"I know, but this one is too big for all of you. Cheer up, I will manage."

"Promise that you will ask when you need help." There was a hopeless tone in his voice.

"I will, Lips, don't worry." I couldn't give them details, but I did explain that there was something that I had to do on my own for a few days.

"Listen, Guys, I gotta talk to Maggie now, so don't wait up for me." Everyone nodded in agreement.

"By the way, have any of you seen Ghost lately?" No one had seen him for over a month.

"If you see him, tell me immediately every detail... where, what time, what kind of car he drives and where he goes, and everything you hear on the street about him."

They were curious and started to ask questions, but I stopped them, "Just do it, and I don't want him to know anything about this, so be discreet. Understand?"

"Will do."

"And don't get close to him. Keep your distance, he is bad news." I said my goodbyes and headed over to Maggie's hoping she would be there. I knocked on the door.

"Alex, is that you?" her voice dampened by the closed door.

"Yes, open up please," I asked while pacing in the hallway.

She unlocked the door pulling me into her arms, "Alex, I was so worried."

Guiding her gently over to the kitchen table, "Listen, Maggie, you know how fond I am of you, and I need to ask you to trust me since I can't give you any details right now."

"Alex, you must know that I trust you. What can I do?"

"Don't ask any questions. Just know that my whole future depends on your help. Lend me your car for a few days."

I knew that I was asking a lot. She would have to go to work on foot or by bus.

She tried to make me think that she needed the exercise to lose weight. Didn't she know how perfect she was to me?

"The car is yours for as long as you need it," she pulled me to her sensing that I needed to be held. Her kisses made me feel safe and forget the previous twenty-four hours. Relaxing for the first time I must have fallen asleep since I was awaken the next morning by the sun streaming through the window. Time had obviously become irrelevant.

Maggie came in carrying a sack of hamburgers, "I thought you might be hungry."

"Indeed I am." The drumstick at Zach's was the last time that I had eaten, and that didn't stay with me long.

We ate sitting on the floor, picnic style, laughing and playing like kids.

It felt so wonderful to just be in the moment even though Simon was always in the back of my mind. I didn't know what to do, but I knew that I would do whatever was necessary to regain control of my life. He was not going to get away with this so easily.

"Maggie, you have been so wonderful, but I've got to go. You are so special."

"Go. I understand. Here are the keys."

"I'll call you later or come by to see you at work. By the way, do you know Simon?" I obviously needed all the help I could get.

"Simon? I don't think so," she said.

I described him, "The tall, dark guy we all call Ghost."

"That creep. Yes, I know him," wrinkling her forehead. Her concern reflected from her eyes.

"When you see him again I need you to tell me as soon as possible. It's extremely important, but be careful and don't let him know that I am looking for him."

"Don't worry, I never talk to him anyway. He's a real loser and never leaves a tip," she lightened the mood.

"It would help to know what kind of car he drives and his license plate number. Just trust me. I'll tell you more when I can."

"I'll see what I can find out. I can feel how important this is to you."

As I kissed her goodbye it felt so good to be so close to someone. The power of human touch and kindness was amazing.

With no plan at this point I took off in the car crisscrossing the whole town wandering through streets I had never even heard of before. I knew that the chances of finding him this way were near to none, but my determination was not lessened. In fact, I felt my strength increasing with the task at hand, plus just knowing now what had created the void gave me new hope.

I had to be patient. This search could take quite a while. The lumberyard came to mind. Better go by and make some arrangements. As nice as they were I wouldn't blame them if they sacked me. Don't want to break the trust we have developed. First thing in the morning I'll go by and talk to Joe. Simon and Zach were still spinning in my head and driving all over town was getting me nowhere. I needed to get organized, check out each street one at a time. I decided to go back and start over with a plan.

Time for a caffeine and sugar fix, I drove to the cafe where Maggie worked, walking in on two taxi drivers having a heated argument trying to get Theresa involved as she effectively ignored them.

"Hi, Alex, what's happening?" she greeted me. The place was packed.

"Not much." I asked where Maggie was and found out it was her day off, and that Rick and Lips were looking for me and sitting in the back booth.

"Thanks Theresa." I said as I walked toward the back. She was snowed under but winked as I passed.

They both stood up as I walked toward them, "Alex, we've been looking for you. Yeah, we put out the word to everyone."

"I told you to be discreet."

"We just said that we had some hot merchandise and needed some help getting rid of it fast," Lips reassured me.

"That's all? Okay, it just might work, you guys, good plan."

Rick hadn't said a word obviously, absorbed in his thoughts. "Talk to me, Rick."

"Alex, I contacted all my buddies, and you know I have a lot of them. Nobody knows where he lives. So I was thinking that we ought to go talk to Peggy in the morning. She may have some information or ideas."

"Good thinking."

Lips came up with another thought, "Hey guys, has anyone searched around the old building where we use to live?"

"Don't think so, but it's worth a try."

"I heard that there's several new kids living there."

"I know someone who lives there," Rick remembered.

"Let's go see him. I've got the car." We all jumped into the car and drove over to the old neighborhood. Since Lips and I didn't know this guy we just let Rich lead us around until he spotted him.

"Gary, come over here!" Rick got his attention, yelling at a guy walking across the park.

He looked suspiciously at the car but came on over when he recognized Rick. "Rick, I see you're moving up in the world. Got yourself a car."

"Don't be stupid. It's not mine, but I do need to ask you a couple of questions. Really Alex here needs to ask you," as he patted my shoulder.

"Who are these guys and why should I answer anything?" giving us his tough guy answer.

"Alex and Lips, they're okay," and as he opened the door a little, "We can do this the hard way or the easy way."

Gary turned around to Lips, "I've heard of you. What a kisser you've got, and they say you never shut up."

Lips smiled and fired back, "You're not doing too bad yourself."

"Can it, Guys! Don't make me get out of the car," Rick interrupted, "You'll regret it."

"Okay, but tell him to shut up," Gary had to save face, motioning at Lips to back off.

"Lips put a sock in it, this is important," I chimed in.

Gary lowered his head. He hadn't known that this was no time to joke. I got right to the point, "Do you know Simon, alias the Ghost?"

"Vaguely, he comes by here once in a while."

This was difficult. He kept looking over his shoulder. I realized that he was nervous talking to a guy in a car so I got out and walked over away from the car. He loosened up and told me that Ghost came by every week or two, but he never talked to him if he could help it.

"I met him about a year ago by the fountain in the park where all the rich kids hang out by City Hall, and figured he was bad news, just creepy, ya know?"

"Exactly." Now I knew where he got his tips to give to Jack to do his dirty work.

Gary added, "That's about all I know, but listen, there's this wacko kid living in the old abandoned building behind the print shop. He knows the Ghost." Rick and Lips had walked over to us.

"You mean the yellow brick building? We used to live there. What's the kids name," I continued.

"Bill, but be careful. He's crazy."

I looked at Rick and Lips puzzled. None of us had seen Bill for months.

"We know him. Let's go find out what's going on," Rick echoed my thoughts.

"Forget it. At night he goes where there's lights and people."

"Why?" Rick pushed. A chill engulfed me as a knowing suspicion invaded me.

"How should I know. We've seen him going in the building in the morning talking to himself. Look, nobody talks to him. He's schitz or something... doesn't wash and stinks. Moaning and screaming until it gets dark then constantly on the move like he is running away from something," Gary finished and backed off. "That's all I know."

"What got into him," wondered Rick, "he knew the streets better than anybody. It's just not like him."

"Yeah, he was the first one to help me and taught me the laws of survival on the streets," I remembered as we got back in the car, "He must be in trouble. We've got to find him and fast."

"Like Gary said 'not tonight'," Lips was in the back seat of the car with his simple wisdom.

"What did you say, Lips?"

"Not tonight, Alex, this is a big town."

We headed home... all talking at the same time, elaborating on theories, developing conclusions, just trying to figure out what could have happened to Bill. We were all shaken.

When we arrived at the apartment, I jumped in the shower to try to calm down. So much had happened in such a short period of time. No sense in going to bed. I was too hyper to sleep, and I could hear Lips still talking about the events of the evening, so I joined them and we talked to dawn.

"I've got to get some rest," said Rick, "I'm working tonight."

"Take my room," I offered.

Staggering to his feet, Rick wondered toward the bedroom, but asked, "What about you?"

"I've got to go see Joe to arrange for a few days off, and then I'm going to find Bill."

"Great, I'm going to lay down." Rick left us at dawn.

$\mathbf{N}$ext afternoon I got up, jumped in the car and headed to the lumberyard to speak with Joe and smooth out things. He was in the office and greeted me, "Alex, what are you doing here so early?" motioning for me to sit down.

"Hi, Boss. I'm in trouble and need a couple of weeks off."

"Nothing bad, I hope. Can I do anything?"

"No, just personal," I answered hoping he wouldn't ask for more.

"Here's my home phone number in case you need it. Put it in your wallet," he instructed.

"Right now, sir. Thanks for your understanding. You'll hear from me soon."

Now I had to take care of Bill, he was in trouble there was no doubt about it, and it was my turn to repay all of his kindnesses. Pulling into the deteriorating neighborhood I went directly to the yellow brick building that we called "the Ritz." What a dive!

I pulled a couple of boards off and slid in sideways suddenly having a bad premonition. I wasn't prepared for what I was about to see.

Walking through the building was an experience in itself, at one time this was my home and now just a few months later I wondered how any of us could have stood it. But now was not the time to look back, I was out of it.

"Bill! Hey, Bill! Are you here?" Nothing but dead silence

hovered around me.

"Bill, where are you? It's Alex, talk to me. I'm here to help you." Luckily I had brought a flashlight that I found in the glove compartment of the car. I continued to call out his name in as nonthreatening, reassuring way as possible since I had been warned of his strange, frightening behavior.

"Bill, come on talk to me. It's Alex, remember we've been friends for a long time," calling out as I swept the room with the ray of light.

The cardboards were still lying all over the floor like it was yesterday. Moving slowly, searching in the dark, I heard a small whimper in the next room where One Eye kept his inventory. There was a stench coming out of this room that was almost unbearable as I approached. It literally made me reel, but I proceeded very slowly letting my eyes adjust to the darkness.

"Bill, it is me, Alex." I heard something dragging across the floor. "Bill, please answer me. I'm here to help."

The ray of my flashlight caught him right in the face. The sight instantly turned my stomach taking all my strength to not turn and run. There was this unrecognizable, hideous form standing in a corner shivering while holding a two by four ready to strike anything that moved toward him. He was tall, painfully thin and filthy from lying in his own waste. What a pitiful site.

Very slowly I extended my hand, "Come, Bill, we are going home." He just stared at me but lowered the board.

"It's me, Alex. You know me. Snap out of it, man, I love you."

I uttered the last three words with all my conviction, but he still just stood there moaning and shaking his head. "Bill, let me help you."

"Don't come near me!"

"Sure. Whatever you say."

"I mean it, stay away," as he raised the board again.

"I'm not going to hurt you."

"They all say that," he said leaning against the wall and lowered the board.

"Yes, but you know me and I came to take you home."

"No, I can't get out of here."

By now I was so close to him I could almost reach out and touch him, so I decided to wait and lowered the beam of light hoping he would recognize me.

"You're one of them."

"No, Bill, it's just me, Alex. Trust me!"

"Why should I trust you?"

"No reason, just give me your hand." I stood completely still not wanting to scare him away and felt that he wanted to trust me. Suddenly he collapsed on the floor overcome by hunger and day after day of not being able to sleep. It all became clear to me as he started babbling incoherently.

"Bill, it's the voices, isn't it? Tell me."

"Yes. Help me." My suspicions became reality.

"You're coming with me." Grabbing him by the waist, I pulled his arm over my shoulder and dragged him out of this hell hole through the boards and into the car. He immediately shriveled into a fetal position closing his eyes.

I drove in silence gently stroking his head. I went directly to Maggie's apartment and knocked on the door.

Not surprisingly when Maggie opened the door she couldn't suppress her horror and let out a scared moan when she saw the inhuman form in front of her. I held the door with my foot and lifted Bill from his waist into the room.

"Alex, my god, what happened?"

"Close the door. Now!"

She closed the door and grabbed Bill by his other arm and helped me carry him into the bathroom. We removed the filthy rags from his body as he just stood in the middle of the bathroom shivering. Then I guided him into the shower, gently soaping him down and quietly reassuring him that everything was going to be okay.

"I can manage now, Maggie."

"I'll get him something to eat."

"Just broth, his stomach is too weak."

"I'll be right back."

She left the bathroom. Bill was like a rag doll unable to stand unsupported, so I eased him down into the bathtub letting the warm water calm him. He allowed me to shampoo his hair and only stared vacantly into the nothingness babbling on about the demons of the night.

Returning within a few minutes, Maggie helped me dry and wrap him in a robe that she had brought. We supported him enough to get him to the table where he sat and slurped a half a dozen spoonfuls of broth. Looking at us with empty eyes he began whimpering. Maggie took him gently in her arms, rocking him like a child. We got him to her room and laid him down covering him with several blankets.

We took turns holding his hand and talking softly to him all night as he struggled with the fear and voices within him. I quietly explained to Maggie what was happening to Bill, but I purposely omitted telling her about my experiences and my search for Simon. I knew it was not the time to alarm her when there was nothing she could do.

"Don't hurt me," he screamed sitting straight up in the bed scaring the wits out of us and then just as suddenly collapsing back on the pillow.

"Man, that scared me," Maggie whispered.

"Me, too." We were both startled by his sudden outburst from within his own private nightmare.

"I'm going to make some coffee. Want some?"

"Yes, that sounds good." I watched as she left the room, then focused my attention back on Bill.

She stuck her head back in just to say, "Thought I would warm up some broth, too."

"I'll be in there in just a minute."

She walked out of the room as I wiped the sweat off Bill's forehead and then joined her in the kitchen.

"I cracked an egg in it," smiling as she handed me the steaming bowl of broth.

"Poor Bill," came out of my mouth as I also thought of myself.

No one deserved the hell he was experiencing.

"Will he be all right?" she asked, sitting the bowls of soup on the table.

"I hope so," was all I could say.

We sat silently eating our soup and enjoyed the warmth of each others company. She returned to Bill's side as I rested for an hour so I could relieve her. There was no way I was about to leave not knowing if he would freak out. After about four hours of badly needed sleep he was terrorized when he woke up not knowing where he was. I calmed him down talking to him gently until he looked at me clearly and said, "Hold me, Alex."

I took him in my arms and simply said, "Welcome home."

Maggie walked into the room and said, "Food is on the table. I've got to go to work."

"Bill, are you hungry?"

"Yes, who was that? Am I safe here?" he whispered. He had curled up like a trapped animal would have when she had walked in.

"Yes, nobody knows you are here but Maggie," I assured him. "You'll get to know her. She's great."

"Good."

"Now let's eat."

Bill was very weak so I helped him to the dining table where sandwiches and hot soup were waiting. After I warned him to eat slowly and chew small bites, he was able to eat a little and then wanted to go back to bed where he slept for six hours with no nightmares. Still weak but feeling much better he could walk on his own and was actually looking in the refrigerator when I heard him stirring.

"I must have dozed off."

"Hi, Alex, can I..."

"Sure, go ahead."

He took the rest of the sandwich asking, "Want some?" It sounded good, so we sat down eating in silence. I finished quickly and cleaned up the kitchen and sat back down with Bill.

"Tell me, Bill, what do you know about Simon?" He turned white and started shaking.

"It's okay. He won't come here. I believe that I know what you are going through. It's like a void in your head every time you close your eyes."

He acknowledged with just a nod of his head.

"It's like you have no memory or feeling, except for the terror of the nightmares and voices always spinning in your head."

"How could you know?" He looked at me wondering how I could know so much.

So I continued, "Remember when we first met how I would sleep all day and disappear at night?"

"Yeah, but you made it."

"Well, I don't know about that, but I'm able to cope," I paused. "Any more than that, I really can't remember how I made it."

"So tell me, what's this all about?"

I really didn't have an answer so I just told him to stay put and that Maggie would take care of him. He wanted to know where I was going and all I could answer was, "Out to find Simon."

"Can I help?" he asked.

"Right now you are too weak. I want you to rest and build your strength, because I will need you later," I assured him.

Bill went back to the bedroom crashing on the bed and smiled at me, "I'm glad you came looking for me."

"You would have done the same for me. Now rest."

It was late afternoon and time for me to hit the streets in search of that lowlife scum Simon. At least I had more information and a place to start — the fountain.

Arriving downtown everything appeared calm, just several kids playing ball, a few couples sitting on blankets near the bushes, several yuppies jogging, mothers with their children, people coming out of the surrounding buildings with briefcases. As the sun started to set the crowd began to thin out and soon there was only the homeless wandering around and a half dozen kids that had nothing better to do.

I stayed for over five hours and no sign of Simon. Well, I struck out this time so I decided to head back to Maggie's place. She would be home soon, and maybe Bill would be strong enough to answer a few of my questions.

Driving toward home along the deserted downtown street I spotted Simon coming out of an alley adjusting his jacket and tie. He walked over to a car with someone waiting inside and took off. I was so surprised that by the time I turned around to follow him, it was too late.

I could see the car but a traffic light turned red, and with a police officer sitting having a cup of coffee in his car at the intersection, I decided it best to stop.

I drove down a few more blocks looking to the right and left at every intersection but they had disappeared, so I decided to go back to the alley and street corner where I first saw him.

Inside the alley was an entrance to a witchcraft store. It was obviously closed, but I knocked anyway. After a few moments I heard the latch click and the door was opened by a distinguished looking, older man with white hair. He looked around the alley grabbed me by the arm, yanked me inside closing the door behind me, took me over to the light and examined me more closely.

"Young man," he said and then paused, "what I am about to tell you must never leave this room. Understand?"

"Yes, sir."

"And you were never here."

"Absolutely, whatever you say." *Was this guy for real or what?*

"What's your name?"

"Alex, sir."

"I thought so. My name is Clayton, but people know me by Clay. Come upstairs with me... we need to talk."

I followed him up the narrow stairwell as I was told into a very large room with high ceilings. It was filled with candles, crystals, and various artifacts I didn't understand. I could smell the heavy presence of incense burning.

"Sit down," he said as he pointed to a chair and a large round table with only a crystal ball and a deck of cards on top of it.

Sitting down I said to myself, *What am I doing here?*

He sat close to me, shut his eyes putting his two index fingers to his forehead. Lowing his hand he opened his eyes and looked straight at me, then he spoke, "Alex, brother of Adam, son of Zachary and Sandra Beard, you have had your soul removed by Simon against your will. It is vital that you get it back, but you cannot do it alone. He lives in a big mansion in a wooded area out from town not too far from your apartment complex."

I slumped in the chair just having had the wind knocked out of me. I was speechless as he continued.

"You will need help, but do not worry, I will come to you when the time is right. Believe in yourself." Another pause, and he dismissed me with, "Go now, young man, we will meet again soon. Goodbye."

I got up out of the chair like a zombie, walked to the stairs, and proceeded down the steps with Clay silently following behind me.

He opened the door letting me out and locked it behind me. I was standing in the alley in shock, mouth open, drained of my energy. *What and who was that?* I asked myself. *How did he know so much?*

Feeling like I was still in a trance, I got into the car and drove away in disbelief of the whole incident.

When I walked into my apartment I got a more pleasant shock, there appeared to be a party going on with the room filled with familiar and unfamiliar faces. Lips jumped up from the other side of the room attempting to get to me through the crowd, "Hey, Alex, over here."

As I crossed the room I took a quick inventory of the faces, I noticed Rick, James, One Eye, Mary, Jeff, Louise, Eddy — all laughing and having a great time. Butterball was chatting with two new girls I didn't know. It was a zoo of smiles.

Lips made it across the room to me, "Alex, how do you like it?"

"What's going on?"

"We've never had a party, and it's Peggy's birthday. So we got some chips and dip and a cake and invited everyone. Yeah, just put the word out in the streets. Isn't it great?"

"Yeah, I'm glad that you did it." Boy, these guys had come a long way.

"Alex, are you okay?" he questioned.

"I'm just too emotional to talk." I guess I must have looked a little or maybe a lot out of it.

"Since it's Peggy's birthday, we all went together and got her a card and some roses."

"You did good," unable to say more.

"By the way I signed for you."

"Thanks, I owe you."

He looked at me directly and added, "You will never know how much you mean to all of us. We all love you." With that he was back to the party having a good time which was just as well since I was speechless.

I rotated on my heels walking straight toward Peggy and Maggie feeling the love and hope in the air. Peggy was trying to get to her feet when I stopped her with a gesture and got on my knees to embrace her.

"Happy Birthday, Sweetheart."

"Thank you, Alex."

"You are more than welcome, but it is all of us who are saying thanks to you." I wondered how many of us wouldn't have made it this far without her help.

"I am fifty years old today. Quite a milestone wouldn't you say?"

"You don't look a day over thirty to me, plus your age is not important to all of us who love you."

She looked like she was about to cry, "In all those years this is the first surprise party given just for me."

"Peggy, you deserve it, and there are many more to come."

"Birthdays?"

"Sure, but other parties and celebrations, and you are invited to all of them."

With that she burst out crying, "I'm sorry, I'm just so happy."

"Don't worry," I said, "It's just raining in your head and flooding your face."

Laughing as she wiped away the tears, she reached over and gave me a kiss on the cheek and another thank you with her eyes.

"Quiet everyone," a voice shouted from the kitchen door. I must have been the only one to hear it with all the laughter and chatter going on so I voiced in, "Quiet everyone!"

The whole gang was there by the kitchen door — Rick, Lips, Bill, One Eye, Big Joe, Butterball — holding a cake with five red candles burning, and the whole room started singing "Happy Birthday to you, Happy Birthday to you, Happy Birthday Dear Peggy... Happy Birthday to youuuu." There was a round of applause as they placed the cake on the coffee table in front of Peggy.

"Silence, silence. Alex wants to make a speech." I could have killed Big Joe for putting me on the spot.

"Speech, Speech, Speech," rang from the room. There was no getting out of this one so I raised my hand to quieten the crowd.

"Peggy, I want to thank you, and I believe that everyone in this room shares my feelings. You have inspired us and given us hope, fed us to keep up our strength and above all we regard you as a loving mother. Peggy, we love you."

By then the small children were pinching at the cake with their fingers leaving the message of enough talk, let's eat.

"Champagne for everyone," Lips announced as he came out of the kitchen followed by three other guys carrying half-filled plastic goblets on trays. As they weaved through the group handing out the glasses to everyone, Lips smiled and whispered to me, "Ginger ale." I caught him off-guard with a friendly jab in the ribs as he moved on.

With all the celebration and everyone trying to talk to Peggy, I grabbed Maggie's hand and led her outside.

"How's Bill?"

"Better, as you can see." Bill was actually laughing at something Peggy had said.

"I'm glad you brought him."

"I didn't want to leave him alone."

"Good thinking," I barely completed my comment when she embraced me giving me a kiss that made my head spin.

"Is it hot out here?" I said stepping back and fanning myself.

She smiled back and whispered, "Get back to the party you soft-hearted tough guy." Slapping me on the backside as I went back inside.

Peggy left early graciously escorted to her car by Big Joe, leaving the rest of us to party all night. The younger kids slept on the floor, and I noticed that Bill had some color back in his cheeks and was joining in just like the old days. As the hours passed by, I sat with Maggie and her friend Theresa talking and sipping our make-believe champagne.

Bill approached us and sat on the corner of the coffee table, "I just want to tell you how much I appreciate all you have done. All three of you have made me feel alive again."

Theresa jumped in, "Come on, Bill, forget it. We all need help from time to time."

"There's another piece of cake just waiting for you, Bill," Maggie commented.

"No more for me, I'm stuffed."

"Good, Bill, matter closed. Right?" Theresa had moved over to make room for Bill to sit down next to her.

"Sure, Theresa, whatever you say."

"In fact why don't you come with me to the restaurant tomorrow? We need a dishwasher."

"Yes, Theresa," he moaned in a tone of voice that made us all laugh.

It was close to five AM when everyone called it a night.

I got up late in the afternoon still puzzled by the turn of events in the last twenty-four hours. The party had distracted my thoughts enough to have a great evening and a good night's sleep. Took a shower, brushed my teeth, gave up on my hair which seems to have a mind of its own these days going in every direction, dressed and walked out trying not to disturb anyone.

It was getting dark so I headed out to search for Simon as I did for the following four nights with no luck coming home early in the morning only to eat, shower and sleep a few hours and hit the streets again. Wandering down every street, alley and surrounding wooded area, asking questions even checking out the pawn shops, I had found nothing. The discouragement was starting to weigh heavily on my shoulders. So I decided to make one more trip around the old print shop, looped by the yellow "Ritz" building, but still nothing.

"I know that I will find him, there is no other way out," I muttered to myself and decided that it was time for me to regroup, so I went by the restaurant to see Maggie.

"Theresa, is Maggie here?"

"She just left."

"How about a ham sandwich and cup of coffee?" I ask.

"No sweat. Have a seat."

I found a seat by the entrance in the last empty booth. The place was packed as usual, so I closed my eyes and listened to the soft music while waiting for my order. Theresa startled me as she placed my coffee cup on the table.

Leaning over as she poured my coffee she whispered, "Alex, check out the last booth on the left."

"I can't see anything. What's going on?"

Cutting her eyes toward the back, "He's back there, the man you are looking for... you know that Simon character."

"Thanks, Theresa, make me a coffee and a sandwich to go, if you will," I was trembling inside as I spoke.

"What are you going to do?"

"Wait in the car and follow him."

"Be careful."

Her concern touched me. "Don't worry."

"I'll get your order to go."

Waiting for Theresa to return I couldn't believe that I was sitting here looking at the back of Simon's head and neck, as well as the man he was talking to. The other man was wearing expensive looking clothes and gold-rimmed glasses. He had grey hair and a well-groomed beard — not a local guy. His most peculiar feature was the look in his eyes — dark, piercing, ice cold, almost inhuman. He made my skin crawl.

"Here's your sandwich," she startled me out of my thoughts.

"Theresa, go snoop around Simon's table and try to catch the name of the man with him."

"He has an accent, definitely not American. Could be German or Dutch."

"I'm going to wait in the car."

"I'll try to get some more information. Alex, I did notice that Simon drove up in a black car with a silver roof."

"Good job, Theresa, I owe you."

"Just pay me back by being careful."

"You've got it."

I grabbed my sandwich and coffee, went to the car, and pulled out of the lot and waited a half a block away in the dark.

I could see the car in front of the restaurant so I started to sip my coffee and nibble on my sandwich when I noticed that Theresa had put a brownie in the bottom of the bag. What a doll!

I listened to a great radio station playing alternative music drumming the beat on the dashboard and singing along with my terrific voice. Suddenly I jumped with fright bumping my head on the roof when I saw that shadow sitting right beside me in the passenger seat.

"What are you doing back? What do you want from me?" I can't believe I'm talking to this thing like I expect to get an answer. "Go on, get out of here."

Well, guess it could hear me since it moved to the hood of the car. Great, I've got a comic shadow. I must be losing my mind not only do I have a shadow following me, but now I'm talking to myself. Maybe I should ask this thing if it wants to play cards while we are waiting. At least I've kept my sense of humor.

"Hey, get off my car or start polishing it!" Just as I said these words the mirage changed its position and disappeared.

Well, I guess it wasn't into hard labor, I thought to myself. *You just can't find good help these days.* As I was smiling to myself over the comical interlude, Simon and his companion came out of the restaurant, exchanged a few words, shook hands and after helping the gentleman into his car, Simon got into his car. I cranked the car and engaged the first gear ready to follow as he was pulling away from the curb. Now I just had to follow him without his noticing me, so I stayed back as far as possible turning off the radio so that I could concentrate. It was exciting never having done anything like this before, actually I had no idea what I was doing. Guess I'll just have to improvise as I go along.

We traveled a highly developed highway for about twenty miles. Then he turned right and continued for a mile to a wooded area. The road twisted and turned as I moved closer — I wasn't going to lose him now! When I saw the lights of his car pull into a side road, I drove on past for fear that he would notice my car, then parked the car about half a mile down the road. As I hiked back to the entrance to the property, I mused, *Wow, what a mansion!* Eight posts on the front porch, a four-car garage, windows and gables everywhere, a solarium on the right I noted, as I could see the plants when I got closer. None of this fits — Simon selling hot cars, jewelry, a crook at best, living in this luxury.

I circled around to the back. There was a deck across the entire back side of the house with a built-in hot tub and grill. No wonder he didn't tell anyone where he lived, especially not us street kids.

A light came on in a room upstairs on the second floor as I sneaked up the stairs to the deck.

I could see his shadow upstairs as I approached the French doors noticing that the door was open three or four inches with a doorstop holding it there probably to air out the room. *How convenient*, I thought to myself, as I quietly entered a very large study. A massive desk dominated the room so cluttered with books that there was room for only a phone and pad in the center.

Four bay windows graced this beautiful room filled with exquisite antique furniture, paintings, sculptures, and tapestries. As I moved toward the door across the room I heard the water running from a shower upstairs, and I felt safe opening the door that led to a very large foyer with an enormous crystal chandelier. A double French door stood open to the dining room revealing an elaborately carved, mahogany table with ample room for the ten chairs surrounding it.

Sweat was dripping off my face as I took several steps toward another double door thinking to myself that it must be over eighty degrees in this house. Pushing the door open revealed the elaborate sunken living room.

"Alex, so glad you could join me." I froze in my tracks, *Where was he and how did he get downstairs?*

I slowly turned my head toward the sofa, and there he sat with the head of a snake resting on his lap. I couldn't take my eyes off of this humongous snake, it must have been fifteen feet long and bigger around than my waist.

Simon was stroking the snake's shiny body. "How do you like my friend?"

"A perfect friend for you," I snapped back regaining my wits while still keeping an eye on this freaky, threatening reptile.

"Oh, come on, he is beautiful. He is so gentle," he added as he placed his hand on its menacing head.

"Well, glad you like him. It can be your bed partner for all I care." I must have insulted him, this sleaze who has tormented my soul for the last three years.

His eyes closed halfway, "So, you are not fond of snakes?"

"What was your first clue? What do you call this jungle beauty?" I asked, trying to keep him talking.

"Slider."

"On top of being sinister and evil, you have a sense of humor. Slider, why not Slime Ball?" I could say no more as an invisible force was choking me, bringing tears to my eyes and cutting off my air supply.

The pain was unbearable as it literally slammed me into a nearby chair and two invisible straps pinned my arms to the arms of the chair. The grip on my neck tightened, I couldn't breathe and could barely hear his words although the sound was louder.

"Listen, you punk, it's one thing for you to follow me to my home and break in, but I won't take insults from someone as insignificant as you. You're nothing."

A white veil came over my eyes as I started to lose consciousness. He must have eased off his choking grasp around my neck because suddenly I was coughing and gasping for air.

"I could easily kill you with my power. But first I want some answers".

"Then kill me," was all I could mutter.

"I'll think about it. Why are you here?"

"I want my soul back."

"Not possible. Yours is special, and I need it."

"Get another one from a dead person."

"I get those too," he chuckled.

"You're a freak." Boy, wrong response I figured out when I immediately felt the choking sensation tightening again. This guy has no appreciation for sarcasm. "Sorry," was all I could say.

The grip loosened. I better lay off the insults and concentrate on how I'm going to get out of this place. Be smart, keep him talking, came into my mind. "Can I ask you a question?"

"Go ahead. We find you entertaining for the moment," he said as he continued to stroke Slider.

"Why did you take my soul?" Swallowing hard as I asked.

"I told you... I need them."

"What do you mean 'them'? How many do you have in your control?"

"Right now, only four. But I have had countless in my very long and prosperous life."

"What do you mean, long life? You don't look old." Got to keep him talking, appeal to his insanity or ego, or whatever.

"Guess my age. Go ahead."

"Between forty and forty-five," I answered.

He laughed, caressed the snake, and started talking to him, "Do you hear that, Slider, forty to forty-five. You gotta' love this kid."

Turning around, he focused his attention on me. His expression had changed, his face had become cruel, his eyes glared with a sinister, ice cold stare. "There's no harm in telling you my story knowing that you are going to cease to exist afterward."

I was stunned for a moment and asked a dumb question, "Then you're going to kill me?"

"Such an ugly word, Alex."

"Are you scared to call a spade a spade?"

"Nothing scares me. Nothing. Everyone must meet his master at some point in his life, and you have met yours. I am three hundred and twenty-two years old, and have the power of the ages."

Man, that wacko could make a fortune marketing his beauty cream, but I thought better of saying it since I wanted to keep breathing. "How can you be so old?"

"The souls I gather keep me young. Let me explain it simply. The mind and spirit controls the body, right?" I shook my head feebly and he continued, "When people say 'mind over body,' they have no idea how right they are. And few believe it. I draw energy from maybe ten souls at a time, just a little at a time."

"You mean like a spider keeping its prey alive so it can feed whenever it wants?" shivering as I say the words.

"That is what I like about you, Alex, you're smart and get the picture immediately without a lengthy explanation."

"Do you have any concept of the cruelty of your act? You destroy the very essence of life leaving only a void and a shell of a body. There is no joy, no emotion left but fear. There is no way to describe the pain and misery."

"So what is your point?"

My words seemed useless as I tried to understand his insanity, "How can you have no feeling when you're draining other people of their lives, their self confidence, their energy, their memories, their very soul?"

"Isn't it obvious, Alex. The power lies in not caring. No one matters but me, my life, my needs, my existence." Simon really believed all this.

"Why me?" as I tried not to sound pitiful.

"Why not you? Plus you have a power, an energy source greater than you know or can imagine. It was necessary to neutralize you."

"What power are you talking about?" I was getting confused.

"Never mind. Now that I have your soul, it really doesn't matter."

"Man, you are really pathetic." Bad mistake. He was offended and tightened the invisible grip around my neck. I continued on with difficulty, "So what scared you about my power?"

"Nothing. We just decided it would be wise to disable you."

It took a second for his words to sink in. "Who is this 'we'?"

"That is no concern of yours."

"The old man I saw with you tonight, does he have anything to do with this?"

Simon was obviously enjoying this opportunity to boast and toy with his prey, "So, you know him?"

"No. I don't even know who you are. My father called you John Languish, but everyone knows you as Simon."

"Changing one's identity is necessary when you are as old as I am. Besides, it makes it more difficult to be traced."

"How can you change your identification?"

"Don't concern yourself. I've had a great deal of practice. And with the papers in my strong box, it's simple," he motioned toward the study as he spoke.

"How did you get by my father? Did you trick him?"

"No. It was easy. He was weakened by years of grieving and anger, so he didn't even suspect."

"Who else have you got?"

"No one you would know, except Jack."

My blood turned cold in my veins. I had spent days trying to figure out what Jack was telling me. It was so clear now, he was warning me about Simon. "Why Jack?"

"Just a bonus, as it happened."

"And me."

"You were a nothing, insignificant zero as you were. Young, weak, angry, unaware of your potential power, it was so easy to take you then... plus by taking your soul we weakened your father's powers. All of which helped me to achieve a higher rank in the organization."

"What organization?" I continued to question.

"You don't think that I am alone? Seriously, Alex, you're smarter than that."

"How many are there?" This was getting scarier by the moment.

"Not too many. But our numbers are increasing, and we are well placed throughout the world. Actually with the use of drugs increasing, our feeding grounds are vast. The individuals are unimportant, but with so many available weakened souls our energy and power grows."

As he was flapping his jaw so full of himself, silently the shadow appeared with lightening speed and hovered above the ugly snake. Simon had not noticed.

"What are you going to do to me?"

"Dispose of you. You are only a body now, no soul, no feeling, no purpose. You are expendable."

The snake twisted and turned, recoiling itself on the sofa and looking up toward the ceiling. Before Simon could react the snake seemed to be propelled off the sofa, as if he were thrown, hitting the coffee table on his way to the floor.

"Slider, what is going on?" Simon asked as he pursued the erratic movement of the snake destroying everything in its path.

The restrictions on my arms and the pressure on my neck lessened, and then were gone. I bolted from the chair and ran for my life through the foyer and study, across the deck, down the steps, picking up speed when I got to the yard. Not daring to look back, I made it to the road and then the car, fumbled with my keys, panicking a second trying to get the key into the ignition, started the car and drove like a maniac. *He was insane, he must be. How could any of this be real? But, what if... I've got to get back to my apartment, I must find them and stop them, I must fight for...*

Floating, what a fantastic sensation, I feel like I am floating on a cloud I'm so light. There's such a clean smell all around me, and the peace and quiet together with this weightlessness is exhilarating. I can see a blurry, bright light off in the distance getting dimmer as it drifts away and vanishes into the darkness. At times it seems to be within my reach. A voice in the background flows in and out of my consciousness just like the light disappearing into the nothingness.

The light is slowly getting brighter, the voice stronger, my vision clearer. I feel so good, maybe this is heaven. I try to shift my body, but it is too heavy and my arm has a sharp pain when I try to move. The room is spinning. The voice vanishes and comes right back.

The room stopped spinning. I could see a form coming between me and the light, a white blouse, the good smell returns. Ah, I'm floating again. Nothing seems real.

"He's regaining consciousness. Get the doctor. Stat."

What's going on? Where am I? It smells so good, and the spinning has stopped. Footsteps on all sides, something on top of me moving my arm, someone grabbing it, white blouse is back, my mouth is dry. I don't understand, my arm still hurts, tears in my eyes, I feel light-headed.

"Alex, do you hear me?"

I can't speak. The white blouse gets more distinct, a woman, she smiles. I blink my eyes. The light hurts now. I try to talk, but no sound comes out. Someone moistens my mouth.

"He can hear," said a voice.

"Give him a couple of drops of water."

"Right away." More water is coming in wetting my mouth.

"Alex, can you hear me?" Same question again. I'm not deaf. A person puts his finger near my eyes. *Don't you pick my nose*, I think, but it's still just a voice inside.

"How many fingers, Alex?"

I'm looking, but it's blurry. I blink my eyes trying to focus.

"Two." Did they hear me?

"More IV, we're losing him."

My arm hurts again. Two fingers dangling over my head. Now I can see them clearly, the light is bright. "Two, Two, Two, Two."

I am babbling, "Just leave me alone, who are you..."

"Nurse, he is coherent, wipe his face and slow down the IV."

"Where am I?"

"You've been in a coma, Alex."

I fall into a gentle sleep. What happened? My mind is awake. I open my eyes, the light is still here, things are clear, the room is still. Someone is looking at me smiling. A man, a tall man, a nurse. The other man approaches and looks at me, "Alex, it's your dad, Zach."

"Where is this?"

"You are in a hospital. You have been in a coma."

My arm still hurts and I'm hot. "Who are you?" It's hard for me to focus again.

"I'm your dad, Zach," the man answered.

"Dad, what happened?"

"You were in an accident. You've been in a coma for seven months."

The words slowly sank in. Seven months, out cold, I don't remember anything. Just the floating and the emptiness. I feel weak again and just want to sleep. "Just go away," I muttered as I closed my eyes.

"I'll be back tomorrow," said the man as he leaned over and kissed me on the forehead before he left. I am so exhausted. I just want to be left alone. I am confused. *Coma*? *Hospital*? *Seven months*? *What accident*? I must stop all these questions and sleep.

The nurses are back lifting me up, changing the sheets on the bed, and then putting me back in the bed and tucking me in. I feel much better. My mind is getting clearer. The nurses are talking now. I must have been hurt, but when? Where? Someone comes in. It is that man. "Hi, Alex." I just looked at him. "You are looking better today, but you are going to need a lot of rest."

"Please tell me how I got here?" To utter that question was excruciating.

"Slow down, Alex. I am here to explain." He turned around and grabbed a chair, pulled it close to the bed, sat down, poured himself a glass of water and said gently, "I will start at the beginning."

I just nodded my head in agreement.

"Seven months ago late one night I got a phone call from the hospital telling me that you were in a serious car accident, and that your chances of making it were slim."

"How did they know?" I struggled to form the words.

"They checked you for an ID, but all they found was a phone number. So they called and it was your boss from the yard. He told them that you were my son, so they immediately contacted me for permission to operate. I got here after they had taken you into the operating room. They worked on you for fourteen hours and really didn't give me much hope that you would live." He paused and breathed deeply.

"Continue, please."

"After the operation I stayed here with you by your bed for a week. Then the doctor told me that it could be weeks or months before you would regain consciousness — if then. We've all come to be with you. Joe comes often. Maggie every chance she gets. Rick, One Eye, Lips, Butterball, everyone comes from time to time."

"Maggie, how is she?"

"Better than you, but worried about you."

"What about her car? I wrecked it."

"She has a new car."

"You mean you...?"

"Yes, her car couldn't be repaired plus she seems really fond of you so I took care of it. Your apartment rent has been paid for the year, and an account set up to pay the gas, water, electricity, and phone. Lips is in charge."

"We don't have a phone."

"Well, now you do, and Rick supervises everything. Lips is the accountant, and they manage very well."

"How can you be so nice after all the horrible things I said?"

"I was hurt just like you, Son. We had a disagreement, let's just leave it like that for now. We can talk about all that later. Just know that I never quit loving you."

"Okay."

"You woke up a month ago but only for a few minutes, then out again. Five days ago you seem to come to, but you were incoherent and too weak to grasp what was happening and passed out again. The doctors seem to think that you are back this time, but it will take quite a while with care and rest to get you back on your feet again."

As my father was telling me all the details, I thought to myself that the lights, the spinning room, floating on clouds had been dreams, but I was wrong.

"Alex, I'm going to go for now so you can get some rest."

"Bye," was all I could say as I faded fast. I didn't see him get up and leave. I was already sinking into a dreamless sleep.

I awakened a couple of times during the night when the nurse came to check on my IV, but overall I slept peacefully until the nurse came with my food in the morning. Well, I wouldn't call it food exactly, mostly liquids. It had been so long since I had had anything to eat even the liquids made me sick to my stomach, but the nurse was patient.

"Take your time," she said.

"What is your name?"

"Heather," she answered with a bright smile.

"Thanks, Heather, but nothing tastes right."

"You must get use to it again. Give it a chance."

"Okay. Give me another bite."

She placed a towel under my chin and pushed a half spoon of stuff in my mouth.

"What is it?"

"Kinda like oatmeal."

"It tastes funny. What else is in it?" *Oatmeal never tasted this bad*, I thought to myself.

"Vitamins, and the rest you don't want to know."

"Do I have to eat it?"

"Just make an effort. You want to regain your strength, don't you?"

I ate making faces which made her laugh. Afterwards she gave me a bath which really embarrassed me. She said I was blushing, but I couldn't see.

"Don't be bashful. I have been bathing you for the past seven months." Swell, that made me blush even more.

Next they came to change the bed. Two big guys moved me gently over to a stretcher while the housekeeper stripped and remade the bed. Then they put me back.

"Great teamwork," I joked, but they didn't answer. They obviously loved their jobs too much to miss a minute of it visiting or joking with the patients. They did turn on the television on their way out.

Boy, I had nothing for almost three years, and now I had my own room, a television, and private care. I dozed off still too weak to concentrate on the box besides there was nothing interesting on. The two happy faces had left the tube on a fitness exercise station, just what I needed in my condition.

Maggie walked in all dressed up looking even more beautiful than I remembered. She was all smiles, behind her Theresa with flowers, then Rick, Joe and my dad. Maggie ran to me and planted kisses all over my face.

"Slow down, you're going to choke him," someone kidded.

"Don't worry. I'll be gentle," she laughed.

What a surprise, Rick and Lips were all dressed up. Everyone started talking at the same time.

"Slow down. I'm too weak to listen to all of you at the same time."

Dad pulled a chair over and offered it to Maggie who sat right beside my bed. Theresa laid the flowers at the foot of the bed as the nurse came to check my vitals. She addressed the happy bunch, "You have only twenty minutes. He is still very weak."

Rick came to me, gave me a handshake, winked and simply said, "Welcome back." He turned around looked quickly at the room and spoke one more time, "Come on, guys, we have work to do."

Theresa hugged and kissed me and left with the others. Dad and Maggie stayed. Dad sat quietly while Maggie held my hand and whispered words of hope in my ear. I could do nothing but smile.

Then minutes later the doctor walked in the room and called my father out for a private talk with him. They both looked at me a couple of times then Zach came back to my bed and said, "Sorry, Son, but you are still too weak for all this excitement. We are going to let you get some rest."

Maggie got up and kissed me and gave me a sad smile, then left the room. Dad left also after shaking my hand. Only the doctor stayed to talk to me, "Young man, you will have no more visitors for at least a week."

He turned around and walked out, and I started to doze off. I remember waking up and going right back to sleep several times not knowing what day or time it was. The only request they made was that I eat some solid food like cream of wheat, bananas, peas, carrots and other foods all mashed up. It was not pleasant, but since I could only eat a spoonful at a time before getting nauseated, it took me a whole week to actually eat five ounces of blended vegetables. My strength was slowly returning, and I could stay awake for longer periods of time.

I grew fond of Heather who was my day nurse five days a week. As I felt a little better I could actually enjoy being pampered. She fed me, changed my bed, bathed me, brought the bed pan, scratched me when I itched, pulled the cover up and down to keep me comfortable, turned the television on and off. She was a jewel, so sweet and pleasant and professional.

Another day started with the same routine, but at least the two big men became more amiable as they moved me around for tests and bed changes. They actually talked and smiled.

"Doing okay this morning?" Heather asked.

"Bored."

"Don't worry. You better rest all you can since next week you could be starting your physical therapy as soon as the doctor says that you are strong enough."

"What therapy?"

"Your muscles are weak so you will start exercising them in the pool."

Well, at least that's progress, I thought. After breakfast I had new visitors, "Just wanted to come by and introduce ourselves. We will be coming to take you to the pool as soon as the doc gives his okay for your therapy. Henry will be your therapist. This is Eddie, and I'm Gary."

"I probably won't remember next week."

"Just ask, we won't mind. You'll be seeing us for the next two or three months."

"Three months. What are you talking about?"

"Well, I'm no doctor, but you figure seven months in a coma. Do you expect to get up and run a marathon? It will take time to train your muscles to work again. We try to make it easy, but it will be hard work. You aren't bored with us at the hospital, are you?" He had a pleasant manner about him.

"Not really, but three months?" I questioned.

"Look, Alex, it took you almost a month to eat."

"I guess your right."

"Listen just be thankful you're alive. Besides next week you get to have visitors."

"Thanks Gary."

He leaned over and added as Eddie was walking away, "Don't mention it. Eddie will be coming every other day, and I guarantee you he will have a joke. So next time he comes in be sure to have a joke ready to fire back at him."

"I won't forget. You two have a great day."

"Will do. Take it easy, Alex."

I dozed off again and slept until Heather came in with a tray of food and juice. "Rise and shine, Alex. Lunch is served."

"What is on the menu today?"

"Same 'ole, Same 'ole."

"Can't wait." I answered sarcastically.

"Alex, don't give up now."

"I haven't given up. It's just that I am tired of the same old stuff every day."

"Alex, chewing is not the problem here. It is your stomach that won't tolerate other foods yet," she had told me all this before.

"I know all that, but sometime I would like to get out of here and have a fat, juicy hamburger, but I don't even have the strength to stand up."

So I ate in silence, and Heather respected my pouting. She just fed me and left after tucking me in. I closed my eyes to rest a minute. When I opened them again, that shadow was dangling over my head. I had forgotten about that silly ball of mist.

"Go away. I'm depressed enough."

It did trigger my memory of that last night with Simon which had been suppressed, but I wasn't ready to deal with that yet. It took all my strength to lift my arm to chase it away, but it just went to the other side of the bed. I watched it for a minute or two and then closed my eyes. *Who cares*, I thought as I drifted off.

H eather had a knack for making me smile. "Alex, tomorrow is the big day."

"Yes, I know the doctor is coming."

"Maybe you will be strong enough to start your therapy."

"Hope so. I'm really tired of this room."

She wiped my face and gave me a light punch on the chin. "Don't give me this silly, pitiful face. You are a fighter."

"How do you know?"

"I heard about your life in the streets from your friends, and nobody knows how you survived the accident."

"Was it bad?" Observing my pitiful state, I kinda' knew the answer.

"One of the worst accidents we had ever seen in this hospital, but here you are still with us and getting stronger every day."

"Tell me how bad was it, really?"

She hesitated. With a frown on her face, "I'm not sure if I should be the one to tell you."

"Explain or I don't eat."

"Okay. You eat while I talk."

She made me comfortable and brought in my food, I patiently waited for her to start talking.

"Alex," she started, "the broken bones, the contusions and lacerations were serious but repairable, but what puzzled the team of doctors were the head injuries. Your skull was crushed, kind of like taking a hammer to a glass, there were so many fragments. Some of the tissue was damaged, of course, with fluid leaking and swelling. Yet with all the damage, there was steady brain activity. With the kind of injuries you received, they were amazed that you lived through the surgery and expected serious complications and permanent damage to the brain. But, nevertheless, you not only survived, but you healed and there was no permanent damage. It is still a mystery, like a miracle. Through it all your father was the only one who believed and kept saying, 'Alex is blessed with the healing energy of the universe.' No one understood what he was talking about."

She paused to get a damp towel to wipe my face praising me for having finished the food and continued, "The team of doctors kept asking him what he meant, and all he added was 'that it was a gift from your mom,' but he had nor gave any rational explanation."

"You mean that my dad spent a lot of time here at the hospital?"

"Yes, almost every day and night. So no more complaints out of you. Cheer up and enjoy being here."

"Yes, my general." I would have saluted if I could have gotten my hand to my forehead. We both laughed, and she left me with a great deal to think about.

The next couple of weeks only Maggie and Zach came to visit me. The doctor gave the go ahead on my therapy, and from then on either Eddie or Gary came every morning, put me on a stretcher, rolled me to an oversize bathtub while telling me jokes. If what they say "laughter is the best medicine" is true, they sure gave me a big dose every day.

Henry was in charge of the water therapy. They laid me down in the pleasantly warm water, and he helped me use muscles that hadn't been used in months. At first I felt like a "wounded duck," but it really worked. After a couple of weeks I was more like a whale ready to cross the ocean, so I thought. My muscles were getting stronger and my stomach expanded. They upgraded me to chocolate pudding still not the real thing, but after a month of the same old puree, it was definitely an improvement.

Henry was a very funny guy, always laughing in the pool, holding me and forcing me to move.

At first it was painful but he did a marvelous job of distracting me with the stories of his life. It was over a week later that I realized that he had only one leg, but that didn't stop him from doing a first-class job with a jovial attitude. His outlook on life was more positive than anyone I had ever met. Absolutely everyone came to Henry when they needed a few words of encouragement.

One day I just couldn't resist so I asked Henry, "What happened to your leg?"

"Well," he answered, "my wife got upset because I didn't do the dishes like she asked, and she chewed my leg off."

We both laughed at the answer, but I understood that it was none of my business, so I never brought it up again. We just went back to moving my arms and legs. Every day I was a little stronger, and the exercise time got longer. I was exhausted after a session, but it was better than staring at the walls feeling sorry for myself.

One day after they returned me to my freshly-made bed and fed me a good meal, I felt strong enough to conquer the world, or at least stay awake and watch a little television. Dad and a man came into the room. "Hi, Alex. I brought you a visitor."

An older gentleman walked in behind him. He was dressed in a classic suit and turtleneck which called attention to his very strong chest. He had white hair like the fresh snow in a field, but walked with a stride uncommon for a man of his years. "Hi, Alex, we've met before."

I could not place him although his face was vaguely familiar. I had also noticed when they walked into the room a feeling of great serenity about him. "Sorry, I don't remember you."

"That is irrelevant. My name is Clayton, but I prefer Clay."

The name rang a bell, but still nothing returned. My dad was walking around the room waiving his arms in a gentle and orderly pattern and said, "We are ready now."

"What is going on?" I questioned.

The man with the white hair grabbed a chair and sat down, pushed one to Dad and instructed, "Sit down, Zach, we have a lot to do."

I don't remember any one commanding my father to do anything. He was gentle, but no one ever gave him an order. With him everything was to be discussed and to be ordered around made him mad, his philosophy was that everyone was equal and had the right to express himself and to make their own decisions, so I was shocked when he obeyed.

"We came to ask you about Simon." Clay started.

"What do you want to know? My memory comes and goes." I said.

"Everything you can remember, and I'm here to help you."

I observed that my dad had just sat and listened and said not a word during the entire conversation. The stranger was definitely in control as he continued, "Don't be afraid, Alex, I know what has happened to you, and we must get your soul back."

"How are you going to do that?"

"I'm not sure yet, but we will find a way."

Maybe it is too late. He has had my soul for over three years now. It must be fading away. I didn't know where those thoughts came from.

"Not your soul, you have special powers which I will explain later."

"So what do you need to know?" I wanted to cooperate the best that I could.

"Anything you can remember."

I spent the entire morning trying to remember anything I could about this despicable character, but for the life of me I just drew a blank.

I was on the verge of telling him to go fly a kite and to get out of my face when Dad interrupted, "Alex, this is very important."

"I just can't remember. Do you think that I'm trying to protect him?"

"No," Clay replied, "but that man, as well as his organization, must be stopped."

"I keep telling you that my past keeps slipping away. I wake up every morning not knowing what will have slipped away, only the most important points are left."

"I understand, Alex, but you must keep trying in order..."

Clay jumped up, the chair flew against the wall behind him. Father and I watched in total shock. The shadow was right in front of Clay growing stronger and more distinct. Clay was paralyzed, his face was disfigured by the terror, but neither Zach nor I felt threatened.

A blue light surrounded the shadow, and it emitted a feeling of tranquility. Clay's face returned to normal as he started to look in admiration, he kept nodding his head saying, "Yes, I will tell them... I will ask... don't worry... I'll be delighted to do that..."

It would appear that he was having a conversation with the ceiling if someone just walked by.

We didn't move as Clay continued to talk and respond for what seemed like a long time. Finally Clay relaxed and turned around, picked up the chair and put it by the bed where it had been previously and sat down. We had waited patiently and watched the shadow fade away.

"Okay, tell us what is going on," Zach insisted.

Clay was smiling, his voice trembled and you could feel the joy and happiness he was reflecting from the turn of events. "It may surprise both of you, but I just had a fascinating conversation with your son and your brother Adam."

"What?" we both spoke at the same time.

"Let me explain. The shadow right here, right now in this room is the spirit of Adam, and he has been protecting Alex all along."

Now I understood what had been going on. My brother was my guardian angel. Whenever there was danger, when Rick was still a bully and had beaten me up, when we heard the news about Jack, the rescue from Simon and the snake, it was all his doing. The realization just blew me away, and you should have seen my father's face filled with laughter and tears. There were no words to describe the emotions at that moment.

"What do we do next?" Zach wanted to know.

Clay closed his eyes for a moment, listened to something we could not hear and in a very shaking tone of voice conveyed, "Adam said he would like to go inside Alex's body if it is okay."

"Sure it's okay with me, but can he do it?"

"He said he could with your permission."

"How can you hear him?" I asked.

"Telepathy. I have the ability and training, but if you let him inside of you, you will be able to communicate with him." He made it seem so matter of fact and simple, like it was done every day.

There was an excitement in the air, but I needed answers. "How so?"

"Well, your lips will not move. It will all be inside your mind."

"I don't understand." I was not sure that I was ready for this change of events.

"You don't have a soul right now, you have a void. So he will fill it," Clay answered.

Sounded logical and sensible, and I was ready. "What do I do?"

"You don't do anything. Adam will do all the work. He said it is painless, just relax and let it happen."

Zach remained silent finding it hard to believe what he was hearing obviously overcome with emotion. He was smiling, shaking his head and stretching his arms into the air silently.

"What are we waiting for?" I asked.

"Lie still and relax," Clay instructed.

I relaxed although I was feeling a little worried looking at the shadow still finding it hard to believe it was actually my brother. But it all made sense, and there it was moving over me. Then it came closer and wrapped itself around me like a blanket. The next thing I remembered was a wave of feelings — love, peace, serenity, hope, forgiveness, humor, compassion, joy. It was exhilarating, then the voice started speaking, and I could not control it, words came out of my mouth.

"Hi, Dad, it is us, Adam and Alex. Come here and give us a hug." Dad got up like a zombie and came to embrace us.

"Dad, we love you, but for now Alex is exhausted so you and Clay must go."

"I'll be back tomorrow."

"No. Not tomorrow. Alex and I have a lot to discuss, but come the day after and Clay please come with him." Adam was talking through me. "We will need each other."

I gently closed my eyes as Dad and Clay left the room and fell into a beautiful sleep with no dreams, no nightmares, no panic, just peace.

When I awakened the next morning, I had a feeling of well-being that I had not experienced in years, and of being truly rested and rejuvenated.

"Good morning, Alex. Sleep well?"

"Morning, Adam." Boy, it felt strange having Adam in my head. I could talk to him without uttering a word, just think it. Even more amazing was that I could hear him loud and clear like in a normal conversation.

"I feel so good, really good, Adam."

"I feel pretty good myself."

"What do you mean?"

"Well, it has been a long time since I had a body around me. Somehow I feel a little more protected and solid."

I tried to imagine what people would think if I told them that my dead brother was talking to me. They would probably lock me up.

"Listen, Alex, I am so glad to be with you."

"Why didn't you come before?"

"The accident in the lake occurred too suddenly, and when I drowned my spirit was too young."

It was so easy to communicate. "Too young for what?"

"To do what I can do now. I was just a kid when I died, and I have learned a lot. I've gotten stronger and so will you. Hey, Brother, we're together and talking. That's quite a step."

I could hear, no, feel a happiness in his manner of expression, "What's next?" I asked.

"First, we have to keep building your physical strength. After that we will have a lot to do together."

"Yeah, it was dumb, you just left," thinking how much I had missed having Adam with me. But now, feeling his presence, things were definitely getting better.

I heard, "Sorry," in a whisper.

"Sorry, my foot. Do you know what we went through?" Could he ever really understand? But did it really matter now?

"Not at first, but when I came back I found you running in the street."

"Oh, that was you pushing me through the night."

"Who else could it have been?"

"Something is puzzling me, Adam."

"I know what you want to know."

"I didn't ask it yet."

"Yeah, but remember I am in your mind. When you thought it, I heard it."

Hey, that's not fair, was my first thought. But my second thought was, *Well, what is it? What is my question?*

"You are wondering why your memory came back as you asked the question?"

Adam knew exactly what I was questioning in my mind so I waited for his answer.

"It's easy. Right now I have my whole childhood memory

which I transferred to you. In addition, I was constantly with you in the street so since I saw and heard everything that you saw and heard, I have your memory as well as mine."

"Tell me more."

"Not right now. It would be too much information for you to absorb all at once, so I will tell you a little at a time."

"Fair enough," I replied.

"Besides, your breakfast is just outside the door. Heather is taking the tray out of the wagon and putting the orange juice on the tray."

"Hey, how do you know that?" Thinking that he was a magician.

"You'd be surprised all the tricks I've learned like going through walls and being here in your body."

"Da, da, da, da... my brother's a spook."

"Watch what you're saying."

"Spook, spook, spook."

"Bing." Something binged me in the head. "How did you do that?" there's great laughter inside my head. Adam was just as playful as ever.

"You're still a spook, but I'm glad you're here."

"How is my favorite patient this morning?" Heather asked, pushing the door open with her foot with a tray full of food in her hands.

"You wouldn't believe me if I told you," I laughed.

"Well, you are in good spirits."

Man, I just lost it I started laughing out of control and since she had no idea what she had said that was so funny, I answered with the only reply that came to me, "Yes, and I can eat for two."

"You're mighty energetic today. What got into you?"

That made me laugh even more. "Heather you are so funny. Come here and give me a big hug."

"Let me put your food on the service tray first." She put the tray down and came over to give me a hug. She was so happy to see me so jovial.

"This is the absolute best I've felt since the accident."

"What is going on, Alex?"

"I had a spiritual experience." Exploding in hysterical laughter, boy, was I witty today. When I calmed down Heather was staring at me in shock.

"Are you sure you are all right?"

"Never felt better. Now let's get breakfast on the road." She lifted the head of my bed into a sitting position cutting her eyes at me. I was smiling.

"Take it easy," said Adam, "you're going to give her a heart attack."

"Okay, but admit it was funny."

"Yes, it was funny, but get a hold of yourself."

Heather brought the tray of food and tucked the napkin under my chin. It was a wonderful moment when the first bite touched my palate, I could feel the texture of the eggs, the taste, rolling it on my tongue and chewing it slowly. It was so good to feel, taste, appreciate, dissect the flavors and textures. The feeling was awesome. I had to share this joy, so I just grabbed Heather and kissed her on the forehead.

"Thank you, God," I said aloud with tears running down my cheeks.

"Are you sure you are all right?" she asked surprised to see me weep.

"Heather, these are tears of joy. I'm just so glad to feel alive."

"But you've always been alive."

"No, it's hard to explain, but I can actually feel the blood running in my veins."

"I guess, we all take little things for granted."

"You're right. That's why we all need to be more thankful and forgive rather than judge and complain."

She just hugged me. She had no reply.

I ate the whole breakfast and felt like a new man. When Eddy and Gary came to pick me up for rehab, I literally jumped out of the bed and when they eased me into the water I couldn't believe how wonderful it felt. Henry knew immediately that something had changed. He didn't have to make me move or hold me or support me. He simply asked, "Your aura is pure gold. How did it happen?"

"One of the visitors I had last night was my brother."

"You seem so happy. You should ask him to visit you more often," he suggested.

"Believe me, he will. But you don't seem shaken by my statement."

"Why should I? If you listen with your heart, the one you love never leaves you." Good old Henry always had the right words, no questions, just resolution.

"Henry, I admire you. You are always so calm, joyful and easy going. What is your secret?"

Without hesitation, he answered, "I just got tired of fighting everybody, judging them, criticizing them, trying to control or be controlled. So one day I said to myself, 'I've got to change.' And I did."

"And what did you do?"

"Accept, just accept."

Could it be that simple? I thought as he elaborated. "Accept who you are and who they are — no more judging or criticizing, no more pointing the finger, no more feeling sorry for yourself or others. Simply feel good to just be you."

"Maybe I should try it."

"It can't hurt."

We looked at each other and smiled. I was so happy to be able to talk and feel the passion of being alive and remembering each word during that hour of exercise. It went by so fast that it actually surprised me when my two chauffeurs came to pick me up and rolled me back to my room. I was babbling to them at a hundred miles an hour. I was noticing everything around me, things that were there before, but I hadn't noticed.

They put me into the bed, tucked me in and wished me a great day. They left and I started whistling.

"Earth to Alex." I stopped whistling and looked around.

"In your head, it's me, your brother, remember?"

"Right, I'm not use to someone talking to me from the inside.

Cut me some slack."

"Okay. Now pay attention, Alex. Tomorrow Clay and Dad will be back so I am going to feed you some of your memory back."

"How long will it take?"

"A few days total. I'll go slowly, you are still to weak to get all of it at once."

He spent an hour or so feeding me accounts of different events in my life, as well as some of his observations. He was right, it was very tiresome, but he knew when it was time to stop and let me rest for a while. He woke me up just before lunch.

When Heather came in I could tell that she was still a little worried about the crazy display of this morning. She had no food. "It will be a few minutes. They want to do some tests first."

"Oh, yeah. I forgot the Tuesday blood tests. Do your job, Master." The lab nurse came in and laughed at the statement I made while Heather got me ready. The little nurse took out her instruments of torture and was through playing vampire in just a few minutes.

"I'll be right back with lunch." Heather left behind the nurse.

She returned in less than two minutes with a loaded tray of steaming food. It smelled so good, I devoured it faster than usual. After lunch Adam came back to give me more information and then my needed rest.

Around five o'clock in the evening the nurse and doctor walked in, he grabbed the chair and sat down.

"Alex, how do you feel?"

"Great."

"That's good to hear. We just wanted to check since the results from your blood tests are way out of proportion."

"Is that bad?"

"Not in your case, but the improvement from last week is amazing." He was obviously pleased as he continued, "Nothing about your recovery has been predictable or explainable. Let me just say that your results are favorable."

"My spirit has been uplifted." Another brilliant quip on my part I thought.

"Just keep doing whatever it is you're doing cause it's working. I'll see you next Tuesday," he said as he turned around and left with the nurse.

"Alex to Adam. Alex to Adam. Come in. Did you have anything to do with this?"

"Who me?" I heard Adam answer.

"Don't give me that. Did you or did you not affect the tests?"

"Yes and no." His personality hadn't changed a bit. He was still as playful, and sometimes exasperating, as ever.

"What kind of answer is that?"

"Well, for you to get better, you needed to believe in yourself, and now you believe, don't you? So what do you think?"

"I get it. Thanks for the push."

"You're welcome, Brother."

I spent the rest of the evening dozing off and on, and when morning arrived I had experienced another peaceful night.

Waiting for the morning chores to be done was difficult I was so full of energy, and I was impatient for Zach and Clay to arrive. But the morning crept by and after lunch, when they arrived, I was more than ready to get the show on the road. We greeted each other and immediately started talking about the information that Adam had given me which took about three hours. Clay asked questions, and Dad took notes. This time I had no problem remembering every detail.

I learned that the older man with Simon went by the name Lazlo, and that he was pretty high in the organization and had to be stopped. They emphasized that it was not my concern for the moment. They knew that Lazlo came into town a couple of times a month to work with Simon. Adam had been investigating their movements on his own and found out that they always met at the same hotel every time.

After I had given them all the information, Dad and Clay left. I was mentally drained and spent the next two days returning to my old schedule of eating, resting and exercising. Adam had warned me that it would be hard on me so he left me to recuperate.

Maggie was my only visitor, and just what the doctor ordered. Our time together was so special, and we even started making plans for our future together. I was even more sensitive, and every touch brought such joy. She brought all the news about the rest of guys — everybody had a job causing them to feel more hopeful and joyful. I couldn't wait to be able to just drop in on them to say "Hi".

The next month I improved so fast that all the doctors came to see me like I was some kind of guinea pig, but they had no answers for the remarkable increase in my strength and vitality. Finally my doctor gave me a clean bill of health kidding me saying, "We are sending you home, because you are eating us out of our profits."

I was to leave the day after tomorrow. The next day Dad, Maggie, Theresa, Rich, Lips and Butterball came bringing me new clothes with the tags still on them. They were so happy and proud, and everyone was talking at the same time including Adam in my head. To say I was confused was an understatement.

"Whoa, Whoa, Whoa, you guys," I said, "my ears are buzzing, calm down."

Everyone quieted down except Lips who kept flapping his jaw wanting to be the center of attention.

"Put a sock in it, Lips," Theresa suggested.

"Like who died and put you in charge?" snapped Lips, but he knew he was wrong the minute he finished his sentence.

"You know I like you even when you are quiet," laughed Theresa.

"Now," I said getting their attention, "what do you want me to try on first?"

Maggie handed me what she had selected.

"Okay, Girls, turn around," said Rick taking charge.

"Do we have to?" Maggie whined making all the guys giggle.

We were turning the hospital into a circus, and it only took a few minutes for Heather to come in and ask us to quieten down. We solved that problem by asking her to join us.

She accepted and Maggie told her that the girls were supposed to turn around while I changed.

"Why should I? I've been bathing him every day for months."

"Lucky you." Both girls laughed making me blush.

I modeled the whole wardrobe even though I needed only one outfit to wear home. My father graciously offered to take the rest of the clothes home. The afternoon was great, but when the gang left, it was really hard for me to settle down and wait for morning.

Adam cheered me up by telling me about my days on the street restoring memories of sleeping on the top of the print shop, some of the stunts Bill pulled to keep me fed, unbeknownst by me, and working on the bumper cars at the fair. He even reminded me of the perfect brownies that Jane made that I liked so much. Just thinking about them instantly made me hungry. I finally fell asleep.

It's morning. No therapy today, but I went to the pool to shake hands with Henry and to thank him for his hard work, patience and wisdom. On the way back to my room Eddie was there to help when I got a little tired.

After lunch, my father came to pick me up. I had been dressed and ready to go for hours. Eddie arrived pushing a wheelchair, loaded me into it and was ready to roll me out to the car while Dad grabbed my belongings. The whole scene was quite emotional.

Half of the staff was at the exit lined up to say goodbye. I voiced my thanks again and crawled into the car. Zach drove away, and I saw the hospital disappear behind us, but my thoughts were still with them.

"It may sound strange, but I am going to miss that place, especially the people. It is a wonderful place of healing," I realized.

"You're so right. I get a deep sense of pride every time I'm there."

"What do you mean, Dad?"

"My construction company built it, and I am on the board."

"You're kidding."

"With both you and Adam gone I went back to work in my company. It's done very well."

We drove along the four-lane highway the rest of the way in silence both of us lost in our thoughts. When the first double iron gate with the carved silhouette appeared, then the second and third shortly after, my excitement grew remembering that I grew up in this area. But it was only when we pulled pass the front of the massive main gate with the same carving in front of the awesome pink stone mansion that my memories kicked in. It was as beautiful and timeless as ever. What a landmark. It felt so strange and emotional to drive back into town after so long. I couldn't help but recall how full of anger and fear I was the last time I was here.

"Dad, I want to apologize for my behavior the last time I was here."

"It was not your fault. Neither one of us knew the forces we were dealing with. We were still reacting to our sorrow and guilt."

"What about me?" in chimed Adam in my head. "I had a monumental reaction and was hurt too watching you two fight like cats and dogs."

"We'll try not to let it happen again," I answered for both of us. "Adam, what if we forget about the heated discussion, and Dad and I concentrate on getting to know each other and appreciate who we really are?" I realized for the first time that I really knew very little about my dad.

"Suits me just fine," Adam responded.

I told Dad about our conversation and agreement, and he was pleased.

Adam interrupted as we entered our home town, "Hey, look at the carillon tower park with the four bells. Remember, Alex, after that ball game you and Cindy making out? First French kiss under the French bells."

"Thanks to you, I do, Adam."

"What are you thinking about, Son," Dad interrupted.

"Adam and I are just reminiscing about the tower."

"How do you feel?" Dad continued sounding like a parent.

"I'm a little tired."

"Do you want to stop?"

"No, let's just go on home. I'll feel better after I rest for an hour or two."

"Janice has been working on the house for weeks looking forward to your coming home. Everything is spotless with new sheets and curtains in your room. She wanted it perfect for her 'baby' boy.

Guess you'll have to adjust to her spoiling you again."

I had forgotten all about Janice, our nanny. She took such good care of us, just like a mom and was a great cook, if I remembered correctly. "I'm so glad she's still with you, she must be getting up in years."

"Almost seventy, but as spry as ever. You'll see yourself when we get there."

It took us only a few minutes to arrive at our house. I sat for a moment looking at the dark two-story house with the gingerbread trim and five posts encircling the half-moon porch. The three wrought iron doors with the tall evergreen tree near the entrance and the contrast of the grey color of the house painted a homey picture.

"Home sweet home," I said with a smile.

"I am glad you're here, Son."

Janice came rushing out the door, running down the stairs and came to open the door. She was already crying and couldn't wait for me to get out of the car so she could hug and kiss me.

"Alex, my little one, it's been such a long time. Welcome home."

I held her in my arms and felt the realness and sincerity of the love between us, I must be in paradise. She smelled like the bread she had probably been baking, and when I looked in her misty, blue eyes I could sense a strength and the resolve to watch over and protect her loved ones — like typical grandmothers of the world.

"Let's get him inside. He's had a big day and needs to rest."

They helped me up the stairs into the house. Dad had moved his desk and a few things out of his study into the living room and created a bedroom on the main floor for me. I was overwhelmed by the feelings of the familiar surroundings. This time I was truly home. I suddenly felt so weak I didn't know if I would be able to take another step when I felt Adam's strength surge through my body coming to my rescue.

Safely tucked in bed I feel asleep overpowered by the mixture of the activities and the emotions of the day.

I spent the next two weeks building my strength. I started walking a little each day increasing the distance as I felt up to it and resting when I was tired. Just paying attention to my body. I had remembered correctly about Janice's cooking. My appetite increased twofold just looking forward to her home cooked meals.

I could feel Adam's presence, but he made the decision to let me adjust and not add to my memory for a while. So most days it was just Janice and myself at the house since Dad made frequent trips to the city. I moved upstairs to my old room. Alex and I were sharing it again. The healing continued.

About a month after I left the hospital Clay showed up for the first time. He was amazed to see Dad and myself out back playing basketball.

"Hey, guys, who's winning."

"Dad, but not for long," I answered.

"I better enjoy my victories, at the rate you're going I'll be a has-been by next week," Dad admitted.

I had come a long way. I was walking with a mixture of jogging between two and three miles a day, jumping rope, lifting weights, and playing basketball with Dad whenever he had time.

"I see you're ready to face the world," Clay observed.

We all went inside for some iced tea sitting at the dining room table while Janice buzzed around serving cookies and cake.

"What brings you here?" Dad asked.

"We are all going to the Big Town to a baseball game."

"Great," I responded, "when?"

"This Saturday. Let me explain," Clay continued. "Zach remember that donation you made to the city?"

"Of course."

"Well, I had your office call and request tickets to the game figuring that they would send VIP tickets, and sure enough we have tickets in the private box with the senator."

"What's this all about?" Adam interrupted in my head.

Clay heard him and turned around to me, but spoke directly to Adam telepathically, "I will definitely need your help."

"I've been ready for a long time," said Adam so loudly that Zach picked up on the vibration and heard it too.

Clay and Adam avoided our questions and suggested that we just forget about it for now and enjoy the day. Just to get our minds off of the obvious, Dad got out some cards and the three of us played gin rummy until dinner. Clay enjoyed Janice's pot roast and left to drive back into town.

Dad and I tried to question Adam after Clay left, but he wouldn't budge. "The matter is closed for now."

Saturday morning Dad and I got dressed, found our old baseball caps and loaded into the car. It was a great day, not a cloud in the sky, not too hot or humid, just a perfect day for our favorite team to annihilate their opponent.

When we arrived, the stadium was already packed. Thank goodness for the VIP parking card the office had sent with the tickets. You could feel the excitement in the air. Everyone swarmed into the stadium like ants into a massive hill stopping only to get their food and liquid refreshments. The blimp circled above with two small planes pulling some commercial banners that I couldn't read.

The gate was packed with baseball fans young and old with banners in their hands ready to cheer their team. It had an almost circus air with fans wearing hats, wigs, painted faces and signs on their bodies, carrying hotdogs, popcorn, drinks and cotton candy. For a moment I flashed to the fair and the bumper cars and Harold and Jane. What a nice time in my life, hope they're doing well.

I hadn't kept up with sports in years, but after Clay came by I checked the newspaper and found out that this was the first winning season in many years with their finest season for our hometown way back in 1977. Dad found an usher who was trying to help several dads with their impatient kids find their gate. When we presented our passes he took us directly to a special entrance for the hometeam locker room. Several of the players and managers knew Dad and were thanking him for something. I was impressed. We stayed only a few minutes.

"Come on Son, let's go up. Good luck, Coach."

We took the door behind us back out into the excited crowd to an elevator which took us up to the VIP floor. There were some security men waiting to check us out when the elevator doors opened. After all the senator was going to be present. We were checked again before we could enter the box.

There are six or seven people already enjoying the buffet and bar with seats for about twenty -five to thirty people. Situated at the top of the stadium over the hometeam dugout, we had a perfect view of the playing field with little closed circuit televisions so we could hear the commentary. The team had moved into the new stadium in 1994, so everyone was commenting on the new facilities.

It was quite thrilling even Adam was impressed, "Is this fantastic or what?"

Before I could agree with him several people walked in the door and immediately Adam whispered to me, "From now on I can't talk to you, and please don't try to talk to me. You'll understand."

One of the men entering was that old man Lazlo with his cold, penetrating eyes. A chill ran down my back. *What's going on here*, was my immediate thought.

"Hey, Dad."

"What, Son?'

"That man is Lazlo," speaking with as much control as I could muster at that moment.

"You don't say." He didn't seem surprised.

"Do you know what this is all about?"

"No, but I'm sure it will be made clear when Clay arrives."

Keeping my voice low, I couldn't take my eyes off Lazlo and admitted, "Zach, I'm worried."

The old gentleman sat down in a chair removed from the other twenty or so other chairs available. I wondered to myself why would someone sit in the very back of the box when there were seats closer to the front to watch the game. Maybe he didn't come to watch the game crossed my mind.

"Has Adam said anything to you," whispered Dad.

"Not a word."

A dozen individuals came in mostly officials including the mayor, greeting each other and shaking hands with the rest. Dad knew all of them.

"Zach, glad to have you with us."

"Good afternoon, Mr. Mayor." Dad responded

"Thank you again for your generous donation. I'm sure you know how much it means to the city," the mayor continued.

He introduced Dad to several visitors, and Dad presented me to everyone. Lazlo got up and mingled with the group. He seemed to know all of them, a real diplomat.

Down in the ball park the fever was mounting with the roar of the crowd penetrating even our enclosure. Vendors going up and down the aisles selling popcorn, peanuts, drinks, team memorabilia. Fans still trying to find their seats, and across in the press box technicians were making last minute adjustments, commentators shuffling papers, talking on phones for last minute instructions.

The door opened with a loud slam, and everyone turned toward the back of the room. The senator entered.

"Mr. Mayor, how are you?"

"Senator, glad you could make it."

"Wouldn't have missed it for the world. Our team's going to make the whole state proud today," he said, spoken like a true politician.

The mayor introduced everyone including Dad, Lazlo, and myself. Then he picked up the phone telling an official that the senator had arrived. Taking his arm he escorted him to the front of the window where the two of them stood and waved to the crowd while the loud speaker announced his presence and displayed it on the big screen.

Clay had slipped into the room during all the cheering, and Dad walked over to shake his hand.

"Zach, I see you made it," was all Clay said.

"Of course, I made it, but I was beginning to wonder about you."

I walked over to the two of them, "Alex, enjoying yourself?"

"Very much, Clay, but what is going on?"

"I'll tell you later. Now, let's go watch the game."

They announced the national anthem, and we all moved closer to the window looking down on the players standing in the middle of the field with their hats over their hearts singing along with the crowd. Men, women, children, all creeds and colors, all walks of life joined in unison with "Oh, say can you see..."

With the last note the announcer added, "God bless America," and the crowd went wild, the stadium full of energy. The umpire yelled, "Play Ball!"

The multitude exploded when the first ball was struck by the bat. Hit high, high up in the air. It looked like a home run but sailed to the left just out of bounds as it came down. What a rush! The fans settled down a little, and we all finally took our seats. The visitors have a one run lead at the end of the first inning, but our team has plenty of time. We all settle down to a scoreless second and third inning.

Then in the fourth inning we have the bases loaded, and the pitcher steps up to the plate. Great, bases loaded, two outs, and the pitcher is up, but on the second pitch, wonder of wonders happened, he knocked the ball out of the ballpark. The fans are ecstatic, jumping up and down, kissing and hugging perfect strangers on their left and right. Our group was not quite so physical, but visibly excited.

We had them on the run so to speak leading four to one through the fifth and sixth innings.

Then during the seventh inning they got a rally going and scored three runs, tying the game at four to four. The box got noticeably quieter, and several people got up to get a drink or sandwich.

I noticed that Lazlo had moved over near the senator standing about four feet behind him with no one noticing.

Clay casually eased over to Dad, whispered something in his ear, and Zach signaled me with his hand to move over to the left. Our team was at bat having just struck out three straight batters at the plate. Three up and three on — things were looking good for the home team. The pitcher got the signal, wound up and released a fast ball right down the middle. Contact! There was a knowing in the sound that tells the crowd that the ball was long gone.

Everyone in the stadium was on their feet. The mayor, the senator, and everyone in the room were standing and cheering. The energy was incredible. Lazlo raised his arms, and at the same time Clay raised his arms and said,

"NOW!"

Zach raised his arms and at the same moment Adam spoke to me, "Raise your arms in Lazlo's direction and pull the energy. I will do the rest."

I felt an immense rush of forceful energy going through my body pulling with inconceivable strength. The crowd screams, the senator screams, everyone cheers. Lazlo screams as he turns around and we all have our arms raised. Five shadows ripped out of his body, his face contorted in hideous pain, his body shriveling into a pile of dust.

Clay grabbed his clothes and threw them under the refreshment table. No more than nine to ten seconds had passed, just long enough for a home run to be scored. I am visibly shaken. Adam speaks to me, "Snap out of it, Alex."

"What did we do?" was all I could think.

"We released five souls," Adam answered with no emotion.

I was shaking all over, "You guys are nuts."

"How do you think we will get yours?" Adam's presence calmed me a little.

"Some kind of warning would have been appreciated."

"Sorry, but it might have jeopardized the plan. It had to be spontaneous, and at just the right moment. Even Clay and I had no idea until Lazlo made his move for the senator. That was the perfect moment. His energy was directed, and he had no defense against us."

"I am traumatized and all you can say is 'Sorry.'"

"If you want I'll send you a letter of apology."

"Good make it soon so I can frame it." Our dialogues were just like the ones we had when we were kids, Adam always wanting to have the last word.

"Now, Alex, gotta' leave you and take care of these five souls with Clay. They have got to be more scared than you."

"Don't let me stop you."

He blocked me out so I could not hear him, but I saw the shadows calm down, listening and eventually following Clay and Adam out of the room.

"Dad, did you know what was going to happen?"

He shook his head, "Not really. I just knew to be ready."

"This is all crazy."

"Listen, Son, these people must be stopped."

"Yes, but..."

"But, what. Do you think they ask permission when they yank the souls out of people? Do you think they give them a warning or decision in the matter?" Dad had a point.

Clay came back into the room and walked over to me. "Sorry, I didn't have a chance to warn you, I just had to play it by ear."

"Next time I'll be on my guard." I had calmed down enough to respond.

"And well you should, Alex. Good job."

The game had started again. We were leading by four and amazingly no one had noticed a thing, people cheering, getting food and drinks. The senator came over to look at the food and grab a drink. Life went on as usual.

"Lazlo will not be missed," Dad said, kind of reading my thoughts.

"How about some refreshments, Alex?" Clay asked.

"Why not?" I laughed.

I asked Dad what would happen to the souls, and he just said that we would talk about it later. I grabbed a soda and gulped it down like nothing had happened. The senator and his entourage were leaving possibly to beat the rush.

Stepping over to the window I watched in a daze the last pitch of the game. The home team was triumphant, and the fans were streaming on the field in celebration. There were lots of hand shaking and patting on the back going on in the room as everyone left.

I realized the Dad, Clay and I were the only ones left in the box. There seemed no reason to get in the crowd as they rushed toward the exits holding children close. In their places they left paper, cups, and boxes for the cleanup crew to dispose of. In fact, the crews were already starting in the nosebleed section with their blowers pushing all the debris down to the lower levels to be collected.

Clay had been speaking to Dad when he turned and spoke to me, "Alex, we hope that we didn't shock you too badly."

"As a matter of fact, you did, but I'll recover," smiling as I spoke.

"It is the first time we have attempted a task of this magnitude, so it was necessary that we be able to improvise and use the element of surprise."

"Well, you sure surprised me," I admitted. "How did you know what to do?"

"The basics I found in an ancient book."

"I'm glad it worked."

"So are we. Simply said we just took all the positive energy available and directed it against Lazlo's negative energy," Clay explained.

"Why don't people use the positive energy for themselves?"

"They forget. It's easier to feel sorry for themselves than to seek out the positive and fight."

"What was my part?" I asked.

"Lazlo was very old and knowledgeable in the negative force, so we needed as much positive energy as possible. You and Adam possess more positive energy than you can imagine. You'll learn as time passes, I'll see to that. Just be patient and trust for now."

"Why did he disintegrate?"

"His body was over four hundred years old," Clay answered nonchalantly.

"That is not possible." Realizing as I responded that I was slowly learning that anything was possible.

"Yes, it was for him. He had mastered removing the souls from innocent, unsuspecting people without their awareness. He would use up their energy, their life force, release it and get another," Clay hesitated. "These people must be stopped!"

"There is more," Adam's voice had manifested itself in my head loud enough for all three of us to hear him telepathically. We waited for the explanation and he continued, "Three of the souls were very deteriorated, so I let them go to their well-deserved rest, but the other two were puzzling."

For the first time Zach spoke up and asked, "Adam, don't keep us hanging."

"Well, one was a high ranking officer in the military, the other a successful business man from a large corporation."

"Where are you going with this?" Clay interrupted.

"Well, I took them both back into their own physical bodies after they had both told me about being manipulated." Adam had carefully picked his last word.

"Manipulated how?" Zach asked.

"After their souls were removed they were asked, or rather instructed, to perform tasks or reveal certain information or they would never feel their souls again."

"But that's blackmail," Zach blurted out.

"You've got it, and you can ask Alex how it felt to have no feeling with nightmares every night. And since they had total control, there was no way to rebel."

"No way to fight," I added.

"No, when your soul has been removed without your knowledge, it is too late to fight." Adam concluded.

I suddenly realized that with my soul gone so long in Simon's control there could be nothing left, or it could be in bad shape, so I asked, "Could it be too late for my soul?"

"No, Alex, you were born with a gift." Dad quickly tried to erase that fear from my thoughts.

"Simon must be keeping it for some especially evil moment in his life," Clay added.

"Charming," came to my mind.

"Don't worry, we'll get yours next," came through from Adam.

"Don't worry you say, the last time I saw him he nearly crushed my windpipe."

"I know. I was there. I was the one who had to toss his snake, and I don't like to touch snakes, even with my soul."

More anxious than ever, I pushed, "So how are we going to do this?"

"The element of surprise. You need to rest for a couple of weeks first. You're still pretty weak," Adam interjected.

"Two weeks. No more. I have you guys as my witnesses," motioning to Zach and Clay for support as I spoke.

"Give or take a day or two," Adam tried to hedge.

"No. Two weeks, no more."

"Yeah, yeah, yeah."

We all laughed. We got up from our chairs and headed out. Lazlo's clothes were left, he wouldn't need them. The ballpark was deserted, even the ushers and security had left. Only the vendors and janitors still busied themselves. The parking lot was also empty. We walked Clay to his car and sent him on his way. Zach and I climbed into the company truck and drove home. What a game! What a day!

R iding home was fun. We talked about our accomplishment and winning the ball game. We passed the white brick church. From there I knew it was only five or six miles home. Dusk was falling rapidly. I was exhausted from the events of the day.

"Alex, are you okay?"

"Just tired, Dad."

"Hang on, we'll be home in a jiffy."

"I'll be all right."

Zach grabbed the cellular phone, dialed a number, and waited for the party to answer.

"Janice, Zach here. Listen, prepare something to eat. Alex and I will be home in five minutes. Thanks," he said and turned off the phone. He sped up a little bit to get us home sooner. Janice was waiting for us on the porch, and we had barely gotten out of the car before she started asking questions. "So we must have won."

"Yeah, by four runs. Did you watch the game?"

"I didn't have time."

"Who told you we won?"

"It's written all over your faces."

I had no reply. I just followed her into the dining room, where a tray of sandwiches was waiting for us. I had a voracious appetite and dove right in. Janice came in with a steaming bowl of soup for each of us.

"What kind of soup is it, Janice?"

"Navy beans and sausage, Mr. Beard, and save room for fresh peach cobbler. One of the local farmers left a basket of peaches on the back porch this morning."

"I'm going to enjoy it." Dad replied.

"Me, too. I haven't had this kind of soup in years." It sounded funny, but was so true.

We paid homage to this well-prepared meal, and I was stuffed by the time we got up. I went straight to the bathroom to take a shower while Dad went to the study. After my shower I barely made it to the bed. I was exhausted by all the events of the day and month. The coma had really wiped me out, and it had taken so long to gain my strength again. Now I was well enough to know that I wanted everything right in my life, and patience was not in my vocabulary.

The sun woke me up since I had forgotten to pull down the shades. I lay in bed wondering what today was going to bring, when there was a knock on my door, and I came out of my daydreaming.

"Come in."

Dad walked in, and sat on the bed. "Sleep well?"

I looked at him still half asleep. "Yeah, Dad."

"Good. Get ready, we have a long day ahead of us."

No matter what I asked, all he would answer was that it was a surprise. I gave up and asked, "Okay, when are we leaving?"

"After you freshen up," he answered.

"Why so early?"

"Early? It is five to ten, you lazy bum." He added that he was willing to bodily throw me into the shower.

"Well, I learned from the best."

He grabbed me, and we wrestled a few minutes before he let me go. I let him win, of course. His ego must be handled gently. I told him so after we stopped.

"I could have hurt you. I let you win, cause you're my dad."

He just looked at me from the corner of his eye, and we both laughed.

He left and I thought how nothing was better than waking up and wrestling with your dad. I got up, quickly showered, and came out all dressed up and asked, "No breakfast?"

"No, we're going to the restaurant."

"Which one?"

"The buffet, all you can eat, downtown." Boy, he knew how to get me moving.

Grabbing the keys as I headed for the door, "Let's go, Dad."

We drove across town. It was always quiet on Sundays, but we could hardly drive around on Saturday when it seemed like everyone in the county came into town.

We found a space right in front of the restaurant, locked the car and walked in. Since it was still early, it was seat yourself. We located a table in the nonsmoking section and ordered our drinks. I got up to walk over to look at the airplane the restaurant had on display. It was made of bent rosewood, but the most amazing thing about this plane was that it could take off vertically. The inventor developed his design from passages he had found in the Bible. The story was remarkable.

"Dad, did it really fly?"

He got up and joined me. "Not this one, it's a replica. But the original one flew one year before the one at Kitty Hawk."

"How come no one knew about this one?" Remembering how Adam and I loved to sit and look at this plane as kids.

"The inventor was bringing it to the 1904 World's Fair, but it was blown off the train. It hadn't been strapped down properly." Dad answered my question.

"Neat machinery," I observed.

"It took twelve years to rebuild, and the second time it crashed on take off."

My mind wondered to the plans that Adam and I had made to build our own airplane. We must have been about ten years old. "I wish I had the knowledge to build a machine of this quality."

"Me, too, Alex, but let's eat now. We have an appointment," was all that he would say.

We sat down and were served by the most charming waitress. The kitchen messed up our order, and she went out of her way to please us. We found out that she had just started working there.

"I hope she stays with the job," remarked Zach.

"I think she will, she seems to like what she is doing."

She came back with our cobbler and a pot of coffee. We left just in time, as customers were pouring in from every direction. I got in the car, my stomach was full. I asked Zach, "Where to next?"

"Surprise."

"Again?"

"No, this is the big surprise."

We headed out of town towards the interstate. Adam decided to pop in and made himself known, "Hi, Dad. Hi, Alex."

The telepathy still spooked me some, but I guess I'll have to get used to it until I get my own soul back and the sooner the better.

"Hey, Son," said Dad.

"Where have you been?" I asked.

"Just in another dimension."

"What do you mean?" I pressed for more information.

"Now that you are used to me in you, I can come and go without your noticing."

"But I don't have the void anymore."

"Yep, I know. I filled it with our memories, hope, peace, and love, so I'm free to get on with my work without you freaking out."

"What work?" I couldn't let it go.

"Are you two ever going to stop discussing everything to its minute detail?"

"No, Dad" we both answered together, which made me smile, but didn't distract me from getting an answer.

"What work?" I asked again.

"Listen, Alex," Dad said, "Adam has things he must do by himself. We can't help him, we can only trust him."

"I'm just trying to learn how to deal with this energy stuff, and how to cope with being a spirit," Adam finally replied.

By now we had arrived at the interstate. Dad pulled onto the interstate, put on the cruise control and headed west. We talked about the game for a moment, then our conversation drifted to our childhood.

"Remember when I took you two to the pony ride for your fifth birthday?" It struck me that Dad must have really been lonely with both of us gone.

"Yeah, I remember. It was so much fun riding the ponies. Adam's pony was gray, and mine was brown with a white tail. We insisted on giving them names before getting on them."

Neither one of us could recall what their names were, but it didn't seem important. We were sharing memories — that's all that mattered to me.

"Remember, Dad, how sick we got?"

"Of course. Both of you ate and drank way too much."

"Yeah, we got sick in the car, and you got upset." I blessed being able to remember.

"I cleaned that car for two days. It still smelled for a month."

"It's your fault, you let us eat so much," said Adam.

Dad made the hundred mile plus trip in well under two hours and was heading toward the old neighborhood. My stomach was getting butterflies. Obviously we weren't going to the apartment but toward the deserted yellow building. I felt anxious, I had had so many nightmares there.

I had found Bill there in a state of filth and totally out of his mind. I remember Lips coming in to tell us about Jack. I wondered why we were going there, but was afraid to ask. Perhaps I was getting cold chills due to the fact that I had recently experienced the cleanliness of the hospital, and the coziness of my home. I dreaded facing the reality of the miserable life I had lived in that neighborhood.

"Alex, do you remember yesterday when the mayor thanked me for the donation?"

"Yes."

"Well, Son, I said I would explain."

"I remember."

"How about when Rick, Theresa, and all the others talked about how much work they had coming up?"

"What are you trying to tell me?"

When Zach turned at the next corner, Maggie was standing on the sidewalk waving at us. She was wearing a new yellow dress with a purple belt and matching shoes. She looked like a model with her hair flowing in the breeze waving at us wildly the minute that she saw our car.

Dad stopped the car. Maggie came over and opened the door. She leaned in and gave me a kiss on the cheek. She got in beside me and Dad took off. She handed me a box that was wrapped with a bow tied around it. She also had an envelope, which she handed me. "Open them," she said.

I opened the card. It read, "We all missed you, but I missed you most of all. Love, Maggie." And the card was signed by all of my friends.

"Open the box, open the box," she was getting impatient. I

ripped off the paper, and opened the cardboard box. Inside was a yellow t-shirt matching her dress. I lifted the shirt to look at it more closely. In bold print the letters spelled, "Glimmer of Hope."

"What does it mean?" I asked Dad.

He turned the car slowly to the left into the narrow street. Everyone was there in yellow t-shirts jumping up and down and screaming.

"Surprise!"

Maggie was hugging me. Lips, One Eye, Gary, and Theresa were mobbing the truck. Everyone was shouting, laughing, clapping. I was more than surprised, I couldn't speak. Bill opened the door and pulled me out after helping Maggie out.

He was about to shake my hand off. "How do you like it?"

My knees went weak. I took a few steps forward. Zach raised his arms, and everyone got quiet. The crowd parted in the middle, and standing there were all the important people in my life — Peggy, Big Joe, Harold and Jane with a box of brownies in her hand. Even Henry, my therapist, and Heather, my nurse, and Janice was there. Wow!

I didn't know what to do. I turned around to ask my dad what it all meant. He was just standing behind me smiling, and holding a purple velvet pillow with a symbolic pair of golden scissors in his hands. He leaned over and whispered, "Welcome home, Son."

The emotion was overwhelming. I blushed, my eyes were watery, truly I didn't know what to do next. Maggie came to my rescue and gently reached for my shoulders and turned me around. Dad came to my left still holding the purple pillow.

"You are supposed to cut the ribbon," said Maggie with a smile.

I took the scissors like a zombie, while all my special friends stepped aside and unrolled a red ribbon. It was blocking a new door to the entrance of the building that I formerly called "the Ritz." It had been totally renovated and looked elegant. I cut the ribbon feeling as if I were in a dream, and at any moment would wake up. But everyone applauded and yelled, "Hip, hip, hurrah!"

Peggy came forward with a piece of paper in her hand. She had prepared a speech. Everyone quieted down.

"Alex," she began, "when your dad found out about your accident, he started to investigate. Big Joe helped him. When they found out about the conditions you and all the other kids had lived in, he was touched. What really impressed him, though, was how you found jobs for so many of the older kids."

"He was also impressed with your getting yourself an apartment and letting everyone come to rest and shower. He heard how you clothed the little kids, too. He decided to go to the mayor and arranged to buy this city block and renovate it. He bought it outright and hired me to manage it. So today, everyone is here to thank you for giving us hope and helping us believe in ourselves again. This building is equipped with a kitchen, dining room, rec room with sleeping quarters and showers on every floor. I've said enough, so come inside and see for yourself."

There was no stopping the tears at this point. This was surely a dream, it was too good to be true. I stepped inside the front door. There was nothing left of the building I remembered. Gone was the dark, moldy, smelly cardboard laying all over the floor. Instead there was a bright, airy, and clean floor that had been waxed until it gleamed. There were flower pots and plants along the side of the walls. I could smell fresh paint. Walls had been knocked down to create the dining room.

The kitchen was completely equipped with pots and pans, an industrial refrigerator, and a highboard for washing dishes. Upstairs the bedrooms were bright and had two beds per room. All the beds had fresh linens and soft pillows. All the windows had curtains, and beside each bed was a table and lamp with a desk as well.

I was so emotionally touched by this transformation that I had to lean against the wall. My head was spinning. This was a wish come true. No, it was more. It was a dream come true.

"How do you like it?" asked Maggie, taking the opportunity for us to be alone as we walked through the building.

"It's fantastic! And you never told me a thing about it during all those months."

"You were too busy loafing in the hospital."

"I had an accident." Stammering like a kid even though I knew that she was teasing, "Nobody asked you to have an accident. So we didn't ask your permission to start this project."

"Boy, this is more than a surprise."

"Don't you forget to thank your dad. It couldn't have happened without him."

"I assure you, I won't." *But how could I ever really thank him?* I thought, as Maggie guided me through the hallways.

Each hallway had a bright ceiling light, and every floor was painted a different color. All the doors were solid wood, not that flimsy particle board, and had brass doorknobs.

"Maggie, how did you guys come up with 'Glimmer of Hope?' That's what you call this place, right?"

"Yes. We had some brainstorming sessions, and one night that's the name that stuck."

"I like the name." *It really fit with the only thing that kept us going when it was cold, no food, and no help in sight for all of those years*, I thought to myself.

"So do we. Lips actually came up with it."

"Lips? It must have made him feel pretty proud."

"You bet, but what really makes him proud is that he's in charge of maintenance around here."

"How so?" I was intrigued.

"In order to give everybody a vested interest, each person has a job around here. There's bookkeeping, laundry, kitchen, and the nursery duty. Then there's our information program, and also security. This gives everyone a chance to contribute and feel needed."

"I'm so impressed."

"We're self-sufficient for seventy-five percent of our expenses. The rest we find outside," she continued.

"Like what, for example?"

"School, kindergarten, plumbing, garbage pick-up, accounting, and legal stuff. The main structure is taken care of by Zach."

"What about money?"

"The city provided a little, and Theresa is in charge of fundraising, and again Zach pays for the difference."

"By the way, where is everyone?"

"Downstairs having a great party to celebrate your return. After all, this is the grand opening. We better go down and join them."

"Yes, ma'am," I answered and added, "I'll follow you anywhere."

She laughed. She was so proud of this place. She was actually glowing. It seemed as if she was floating on air. I couldn't resist and took her in my arms, kissed her, and said, "I love you, Maggie."

"Hey, hey, hey, behave yourself," Adam was talking in my head.

Meanwhile Maggie was blushing and hugging me around my neck. "Alex, we were so worried about you when we found out about the accident. The first time I saw you in the coma, I cried. To see you here now, I won't ever let go of you, again."

"You are hooked, brother?"

"Don't get jealous, Adam, or I'll block you out. Do you hear?"

"Don't waste time talking to me, kiss her again."

I took his advice. I then put my arm around her waist, and we walked down to the dining room.

The party was going strong. Everybody was having a good time. The radio was blaring, but thankfully in this neck of the woods we weren't about to disturb anybody. Most of this neighborhood had been deserted for the past ten years. It looked like we might be bringing some new blood into the area.

Maggie and I joined the crowd. I met Big Joe's wife, who was almost a foot taller than him. "Alex, I want you to meet my wife, Alice."

"Pleased to meet you, ma'am."

"Me too. I heard you worked for Harold, and Jane is a dear friend of mine."

"Yes, ma'am. I had a wonderful time with them. They gave me the will to fight and to live again."

"They are pretty fond of you, too."

I kept mingling. Each person wanted to know how I was or to thank me. Dad was also getting his share of appreciation and hero worship, which was well-deserved. I needed to have a serious talk with him once everything was over.

Lips came over to thank me. "How does it feel to be a hero to everyone?"

"Great," I replied, uncomfortable with the attention and changed the subject quickly. "I hear congratulations are in order, Lips. I heard about you being in charge of keeping the place clean."

"Yep, and clean I will keep it."

"How many do you have working with you?"

"There are four of us. We clean the hallways, bathrooms, and kitchen. Everyone does their own bedrooms. We sweep the sidewalk every morning, empty the garbage, and clean the rec room."

"Enough, enough. I understand," I said laughing.

"Is he bothering you?" Bill had snuck up behind me and put his hand on my shoulder.

"Bill, what are you up to these days ?"

"Not much. I still have the nightmares, and the fear, but I have complete confidence that it's going to get better with all of you around me."

"Now that I'm better, I can help you more."

"Appreciate it, man. I see you're doing fine." Bill had come a long way.

"Never better." What a wonderful feeling being back with my friends.

"Maggie is a fine girl. You better take good care of her and treat her right, or I'll come after you," Bill said laughingly while squinting his eyes to look threatening.

"Beat me up, right."

"Something like that."

"So tell me, what is your task in the building?" I asked Bill.

When given a chance, Bill could talk as well as the best. He told me that he mainly worked outside of the center going from business to business asking if they had any jobs available. Then he would take the kids over to fill out applications and help them get started.

"What kind of response do you get?"

"Great, I must say. The whole city has heard of your dad's donation and people don't want to get left out, so they give us a chance."

"You do this alone?"

"No. James helps me. He's a little older, but I do most of the talking," pausing to get his breath he rushed on, "we make a good team. He gets us in the door and I tell them about life on the street and how crime will decrease with people getting jobs. Did you hear about One Eye?"

"No, what happened?" Perhaps showing a little concern in my question.

There was pride in Bill's voice as he talked about himself and One Eye, "Don't be alarmed. Remember Thomas, the old man who owned the old print shop?"

"You mean where all of us lived up above the shop in the air conditioner structure?"

"That's the one. Well, he retired not too long ago since there wasn't enough work. Zach came in and bought the shop and cleaned it up. He added some new machines as well and asked Thomas to reopen the print shop and teach us a trade. One Eye is chief editor."

"You're kidding."

"No, Thomas gave him an old leather visor that reads 'Editor' across it. It's old and worn out, but One Eye wears it every morning. He gets to the shop before Thomas to set up the machines. Then at nine AM they start working."

"What do they print?" I asked.

"All sorts of great stuff." Bill continued, "Pamphlets on how to survive in the street, where to get help, how not to get pregnant, how to get your GED, just to name a few. We also print information on diseases, drug prevention, who to call if you're abused, where to find food and shelters, how to apply for jobs, and lots of other things. We even have a little book of hope and self-esteem, and it's all for free."

"Man, that is great."

"Yes, but the thing I like best is the fact that 'Glimmer of Hope' is never closed. We have a room on the main level where you can shower regardless of who you are or what time it is."

These guys had thought of everything. Bill was on a roll and proceeded to tell me about the "wash your clothes while you wait" service. Robes were even available until the clothes they wore in were washed and dried.

"What a great idea!" I was impressed and asked, "Who thought of that?"

"Theresa. She's really committed to this place," Bill showed his pride as he mentioned her name.

"How is she doing?"

"Great. She works outside, plus some at the shelter.."

"I heard you two were going out together."

"Yeah, we've been dating for the last four months."

"She has such poor taste." Slapping him on the back.

"What can I say? Love makes you blind."

"I'm glad you two are happy."

"Let me introduce you to Thomas. He's wanted to meet you

and I see him near the door."

We walked over to an older gentleman with thinning grey hair. He had red cheeks and big ink-stained hands, probably from all those years working the printing press. "Thomas, I want you to meet someone."

He turned around and said with a twinkle in his eyes, "Bill, it's good to see you." Then asked, "Are you having a good time?"

"Just great, Thomas. I wanted to introduce you to Alex."

Extending my hand to this gentle man, it amazed me that I had never actually seen this man in all those years. "Pleased to meet you, Sir."

"Me, too. Please call me Thomas."

"Mighty nice of you to come out of retirement and teach us how to operate all the printing machines."

"Oh, it's good for me too. I was getting bored with staying home all the time. I've heard a lot about you, young man." Thomas had a peacefulness about him as he spoke.

I felt really comfortable with the man, "You probably know now that we used your roof for a home."

"Yes, but I still don't understand why you didn't ask me for a little help."

"We street kids don't like to ask. Kinda' tired of hearing no, and most of us have been deceived or disappointed by parents or grown-ups. We learn to quit trusting and are actually afraid of adults," I tried to explain.

He looked puzzled, "How could we scare you?"

"We don't want to be deceived again. Plus we see a lot of adults say one thing and do another." I sensed he understood what I was trying to say.

"I understand. I grew up during the war," he added.

"Then you understand why we were confused, but also why it's so vital that for us to learn to trust each other again." And I thought to myself, *It was like a war in the streets.*

"That is the reason I came back to the print shop. I wanted to make a difference, even if it was a small one."

"How is One Eye doing?" I asked.

"He's a very good student. He never misses a day. He's always punctual, and I have to kick him out at the end of the day or he'd stay and work all night."

"One thing I'll say about him is that he'll never let you down."

Maggie had walked up to us. "Excuse me. Alex, Peggy wants to talk to you."

"Coming Maggie. Nice to have met you, Thomas."

"Likewise, Alex." We shook hands as I turned to leave.

"Thanks to you and your dad, maybe we can change things for the better." He had the right idea.

We worked our way over to Peggy, but not without getting stopped a few times to say hello to folks. There were so many happy people. Big Joe and Harold together with Gary had started the barbecue. There was sausage, chicken, burgers, and hotdogs. On a side table some of the girls were preparing a giant salad, and Jane brought the pastries. She'll make us all fat, as I sized up the brownies.

Rick had returned in a van that had "Glimmer of Hope" printed in gold letters across the sides and back. He opened the side door and lifted out a tasty looking cake. Two kids ran over to help him. Everyone wanted a piece before the main course.

Peggy was moving toward me, "Alex, how do you like this?"

"Absolutely unbelievable."

We stood arm-in-arm in silence watching the festivities.

"Your dad came one day after he bought the building and asked me if I wanted to be in charge of the center. He really caught me off guard, and I told him no at first."

I couldn't believe it, and asked, "Why? You are perfect for it and I know you've worked for years to help get us kids off the streets."

She caught me off-guard with her answer, "I didn't think I could do it."

"Peggy, you can do anything. You told me so yourself," I reminded her.

"I realized that with the help of some of the youngsters, and your dad wouldn't take no for an answer. We're doing all right as you can see, and I couldn't be happier."

"How can I help you, Peggy?"

"I have a couple of kids from one of the gangs that want to get out, but they're scared of the gang leaders."

"I'll talk to my dad about it, and I'll see what I can do."

She continued, "They just need another street kid to talk to them and help them feel strong."

"We'll talk some more when I come back in a couple of days."

"We have a room here just for you. It's there for you anytime."

"Peggy, you're the best." There was a thank you in the hug that I gave her.

"BARBECUE'S READY! COME AND GET IT!" shouted Gary. He was as jovial as usual with an oversize fork in his hand, waving it in the air as he spoke.

The rush was on. Folks grabbed the paper plates, plastic forks, and started in on the food. Hunger was evident. The children were all over the place, while the older folks waited patiently until things calmed down a little.

"Alex, your brother's here, back in your head," I heard Adam say.

"I'm not speaking to you. You never told me about this wonderful project."

"And ruin the surprise? You've got to be kidding!"

"To be honest, I'm glad you and Dad surprised me," I admitted.

"Zach had a lot to do with it."

"It looks like he had everything to do with it."

"You did most of it by believing in yourself. Then you took it one step further by letting others stay at your place, and helping them find jobs."

Zach walked up next to me, "Talking to your brother, are you now, Alex?"

"How much have you invested in this project?"

"Irrelevant, isn't it?" That was a typical answer coming from Dad.

"Of course, but do you have enough to pay for all of this?"

He looked a little uncomfortable talking about money, "I have enough to do a lot of good, and then some."

"But we live in a small town in a small house."

"Well, Alex, the roof doesn't leak, and there's always hot food on the table. Isn't that enough?" His logic was perfect.

"I guess so. I'm just surprised."

"Do you want me to put an ad in the paper and tell the world our financial status?"

"Stop joking."

"Well, I decided a long time ago that you and Adam should grow up simply and not have to worry about anything. I did the best that I could and we still had our problems. Now I have the resources to help other kids, and so I feel privileged to be able to be of assistance. You actually got all this started, all I did was give it a little push and financial backing."

"I never realized how much you loved us, Dad."

"I know I didn't show it all the time. I was busy and distracted more than I realized at the time, or maybe my priorities were a little out of balance."

"Well, you've done good," I said as I hugged him. "Now, let's eat some cake."

Dad and I joined the rest of the crowd, and the remainder of the afternoon was a total success. I didn't have a worry in the world. The reality of the street was forgotten, and for a few brief hours everyone relaxed and acted like loving human beings, their real selves.

Maggie was sitting at one of the tables in her yellow outfit and smiled when she saw me. Lips had a group listening to his stories, and Rick was singing along with the radio. Bill and Theresa joined in. None of them could carry a tune to save their lives, but it didn't matter. Harold was sipping a cup of coffee, and I grabbed the opportunity to go and talk to him, since I hadn't had a chance to say a word to him and Jane.

"Harold, you made most of this possible."

"Alex, you did it yourself." We hugged with mutual love and respect..

"I must have looked pretty scruffy when you first saw me."

"No kidding, but your smile seemed sincere."

We walked over to some empty chairs. "How is the bumper car business?"

"Don't know."

"What do you mean?"

"I got diagnosed with cancer, nothing terminal, but I thought, 'Why not take a break?' Now I devote my time to Jane and living every day to it's fullest."

"She must be glad, and good for both of you."

"Well, no one will take care of me but myself. Even lost some weight"

"So now you just travel around?"

"Yes. I bought a small RV and got a 1-800 number so my

family can contact me. The rest of the time we are going where it's warm in the winter and cool in the summer. We found this place in the north country for the summertime. It's in this incredible forest, and I do a lot of trout fishing." There was pleasure in his every statement.

"You've got it all figured out."

"I spent thirty-one years in the bumper ride business. Don't you think Jane deserves my undivided attention for a while?"

"Hey. Go for it and make her happy. Looks like it agrees with you, too."

We talked about the five weeks we spent satisfying all the customers. I asked about the other ride owners, and how they were doing. He insisted that I take his beeper number and to call if I ever needed any help. I said I would call even if I didn't need his help. I wanted to stay in contact with him and Jane.

They were the turning point for me, and I'll never forget them, and wanted to have them in my life, even if they didn't live here. He gave me a warm handshake before they left.

Dusk was falling. All the children had been taken inside, and the volunteers were helping them get ready for bed.

We started folding the chairs and taking down the tables. Others put the food away and cleaned up the remaining paper plates and trash. Butterball got a broom, and Lips followed behind with a trash bag. In less than an hour the place was spic and span again.

There were people sitting in groups, talking about the day and how much fun they had had. I sat down on an ice cooler, and Big Joe came over.

"I gave your job away."

"No sweat, I'm still not in shape to get back to work."

"The yard is expanding, so I asked Rick to bring a few young lads to apply. I'm promoting him to supervisor. He's going to be in charge of hardware. He'll be restocking, cutting the chains, finding the right screw or bolt. He really likes the challenge."

"Hope he likes the advancement."

"Well, he's been hounding me for the last two months," Big Joe laughed.

"Alex, we need to be leaving." Dad had walked up.

"Be right with you, Dad."

"How are you doing, Zach."

"Joe, can't complain, and you?"

"Great! We don't see you around very much anymore. Missy would like to have you both over to the house for dinner."

"Call me, and we'll set a date."

"I'll do it next week."

"Come on, Alex it's getting late."

We said our goodbyes to everyone before heading back home. We were back to the highway leading to our little town. "Dad, Peggy approached me about two street gang members that want to get out of the gang. It's just that they are afraid of the consequences if they do."

"When do you want to take care of it?"

"You don't mind?"

"No, not as long as you take someone with you. And I don't mean Adam. I mean someone physical."

"You're making jokes."

"Yes, but I mean take someone with you."

"Who do you suggest?"

"If you do it in the next couple of days, Pat or I will come with you."

"Pat?"

"Pat McGill. You know, he used to come to the house all the time."

"Don't remember."

"You saw him at the yard. He's the one who told me you were working there."

"Now I recall. Why don't we do it toward the end of the week?"

We drove back into town. The large brick house on the main street was all lighted up. They must have been having a celebration of some sort. It looked nice with the eight brick columns, four on each side of the entry way decorated with tiny lights encircling each column. They had built two balconies that covered the front porch. People were coming in and out of the porch door and the other side entrance. Gentlemen in black ties had their glasses raised for a toast, and ladies in long gowns stood by chatting. The balconies were visible due to spot lights pointed upward, and the widow's walk was decorated with more tiny white lights giving the house a castle effect. It looked so elegant. We turned and drove by the park and then past the gazebo with the duck on top downtown. We were both pleasantly exhausted as we arrived home after stopping for some milk for breakfast.

A knock at the door brought me out of my daydreaming. "Come in."

"Alex, could you come out and meet me in the study? I have a lot of work to do and I could use your help."

"Be right there, Zach."

I slipped out of my robe to put on some jeans and a light t-shirt. I walked downstairs into the study, where Dad was sitting at his desk. It was almost completely cleared off, except for a couple of frames with pictures of Adam and me. The telephone was off to the side. I looked around the rest of the room. It was almost empty as well. Gone were the stacks of paper, books, and magazines.

"Sit down Alex. There are a quite a few things that need to be cleared up."

I sat quietly in the recliner, while Dad seemed to gather his thoughts. He sighed and seemed a little anxious as well, "There's a lot I have to tell you, but feel free to interrupt and ask questions."

"Before we start, where is Adam?" I asked.

"Adam's soul is inside you, but the essence of his spirit can come and go. You have your own life to lead, and he doesn't want to intrude all the time."

"So he's not here right now."

"No. He left you enough of his soul to fill the void in your heart. He replaced feeling, memory, love, forgiveness, and if he thinks you need him or you are in danger, he will automatically return."

"I'd been wondering about that. Sometimes we can talk, and other times he just disappears. Now it makes more sense."

"Let's go back to the beginning. For a long time, even before I met your mother, I had been involved in the consciousness movement. It focused on loving everyone without judgement, helping each other, self awareness, directing the energy of the universe to the betterment of others and oneself. I met your mother, Sarah, at one of these meetings. We began seeing each other, and as our love grew, we made plans to spend the rest of our lives together."

After a pause he continued, "Later I found out that your mother had special powers, more powerful than anything I had ever encountered. She rarely talked about it, but she always made sure she surrounded herself with a shield of energy. When it was up and around her, she was calm and serene, but when she got sick and couldn't keep the shield up, she was nervous and anxious. No, even more than that, she was downright scared."

"So one day I asked her what it was all about. What she told me came as an avalanche and left me dumbfounded for a long time. She had been part of an organization of people with interests similar to hers that were developing or researching ways to control weaker spirits without the person realizing what was happening. The person would just suddenly start experiencing fear and not much else. These people could take a soul either by being with the person or over the phone using hypnosis. Your mother was a part of this, but eventually she couldn't cope with the way they were using their power and questioned their goals. One day she decided to leave, knowing it wouldn't be easy and that they would never stop hunting for her."

"To protect herself, she put up a shield of energy, and by doing so she was safe and they couldn't find her. Your mother and I shared twelve very special years. During that time I met Clayton. He became a good friend. He also became my mentor, and I learned a whole lot from him about metaphysics. Slowly I let my guard down and told him about the secret organization. Turns out that Clay had heard of them, but no one ever knew where they were or how they operated. With time, Clay and I forgot about it, but your mother never let up her vigilance. I guess Clay and I just couldn't grasp the magnitude of their power to destroy people's lives."

"One day your mom came home with the second most beautiful news in the whole world. She was pregnant."

"Zach, what was the best news in the world?"

"Later when she told me she was going to have twins."

Now that made me smile. No matter how serious Dad was, he always had a way to bring a smile or laugh into the flow of conversation.

"I felt so proud about the good news, I immediately took off one week. We flew to a private resort and had a great time. Upon our return, I decided to become less of a work-aholic. I would take off two days a week to spend quality time with her. I can't tell you what happened, because I'm not sure myself, but she must have let her guard down. That part still puzzles me, how it was they got a hold of her. In any case, she started to experience the fear again. She never let it interfere with our life. All she would say was that no matter what happened, her love would always be with me. I still feel it today."

"On the day you and Adam were born, your mom was in the middle of labor. We had just moved her to the delivery room. Her contractions were continuous. She was close to giving birth. She delivered Adam, and you followed minutes later. We were so happy, but your mother was quite drained. An intern appeared, and moved from the left side of her to her right side and very lightly raised his arms. I didn't know it, but he drained her of her last energy. Your mom suddenly turned white, clutched my hand, and drew me down to her. She looked at me with sad eyes. The life was draining out of her, and it scared me. She whispered the words, 'Take care of the children. You know I will love you forever.' And then she was gone, just like that."

The heart monitor went off and was screaming. Everyone was trying to bring her back. The intern slipped out the door. He looked back one more time, and I caught his eye. I will never forget what he looked like, and I spent years keeping my eyes open for him. When you were in the hospital and were describing the eyes of the man sitting with Simon, I knew it was the same man. Lazlo had drained the life out of my Sarah."

I was in the recliner shaking. A cold sweat was running down my back. That no good animal had killed my mom, depriving us of her forever. The anger was mounting.

"Alex, snap out of it!"

"How did you find him again?"

"I didn't. It was Adam while he was protecting you."

"So he knew who that man was."

"Not really. Adam came when I was with Clay and communicated with him. So when you were following Simon, we were already after Lazlo. Your impatience almost blew up everything by going to see him by yourself. Luckily, Adam was watching over you."

"I guess so."

"Now you understand why we were not remorseful about terminating Lazlo at the ballpark."

"But you told me he was powerful, yet he put up no resistance."

"He was concentrating his energy elsewhere, so we got him by surprise."

"What happened with the five souls you released?"

"Actually, there were eight, but three of them were so consumed they faded upon release. Three of the other ones were battered beyond repair, and Adam took them. He showed them the way to the other dimension, where they will get a well deserved rest. The remaining have consented to help us fight this evil organization, but that will take time."

"If they are back in their bodies, won't the organization know?"

"The two remaining souls are not in their bodies, but in the other dimension. Like Adam, they left enough behind to fill their own void, but can also keep communicating, like Adam does with you. Adam stays in contact with them, and all of them are gathering information."

"That is all well and good, but I still want my soul as soon as possible."

"We will get to that matter next week. Don't worry, your spirit has not suffered. You and Adam were born with Sarah's power and access to the energy of the universe."

"But why take my soul?"

"To punish us for Sarah's betrayal by leaving the organization."

"They're going to be really upset when they find out we zapped one of their best," I thought out loud.

"It's a chance we took, and since we caught him off guard I don't know if they actually know who did it."

"Hope not, otherwise we will have to learn to duck big time."

We took a pause. I had so many questions. "Zach, why didn't you tell me about my mother earlier?"

"What for? You were busy growing up, and you wouldn't have understood. Besides, I had looked for the man with ice cold eyes for fifteen years and never found him."

"I guess you're right." None of this would have been believable three years ago.

Sitting quietly for a minute he added, "You know, your mother would be proud and liked what you've done with your life."

"She probably knows. Maybe Adam is talking to her from time to time."

"I hope so, Son. Listen, Alex, I'm going to straighten up the basement. Care to give me a hand?"

"Can do. How come you've straightened up the study? It looks so spacious now."

"I see that you noticed. Well, I decided to air out the place a little. I've gotten over the past, and I want to get on with my life." He stood up, looked around the room, and smiled. "So I'm getting rid of some of the knick knacks and unwanted memorabilia."

It was heart warming to relate to my dad — man to man. "Good. Let's go down to the basement."

"Well, I'm going to grab me a soda. You want one, son?"

"Yes, Dad, grab me an apple too, when you are in there."

I went to the basement door and turned on the light and walked down the stairs and looked around. Boy, this basement was cluttered. "Where do we start?" I wondered.

Dad was not far behind me with two sodas in his hand, struggling with the apple and a book under his arm.

"Dad, where do you want to start. Gasoline and a match?"

"You are really funny. I asked you to help me, not destroy the place."

"Just kidding. But look around, it all looks like junk."

"You should know. Most of it is your toys. Some of it is work related, and a couple of those boxes are filled with photographs."

"What is the book under your arm?"

"Just a book I meant to bring down a long time ago."

We opened the cans of soda, shared the apple, and started to move the business related boxes by the entrance. Dad had just enlarged his office and had more storage space in the city.

"Pat is supposed to come by and load up all of the business records around four this afternoon." These boxes accounted for two thirds of the basement.

"I hope he's got a dump truck or van or something," I commented.

"He's bringing the company van. We'll load tonight and take the business boxes to the office before he comes back to get the rest tomorrow."

"Look, Zach, I found some pictures."

"Let me see what you've got." There were pictures of him and Sarah and some of me and Adam, too. "I don't think I really want to look through them again, Alex. The pictures of Sarah still make me sad."

"Aw, come on, Dad, she was my mom after all, and I want to know more about her."

"All right, if you insist. Hand me a few."

I must admit, it was the best afternoon in my life. I learned so much about Mom. I learned about her kindness and patience. He told me how he met her, how they went horseback riding in the hills. He described how they would look into each others' eyes for hours, holding hands and not speaking. Words weren't necessary.

In the silence of the night lay their poetry. He would wake up early, before her and go down and make her coffee. He'd go get a fresh flower in the garden and put it on the tray and go back upstairs. Then he would tickle her with the flower on her ear until she woke up.

One day she told Dad to be home early, because she wasn't feeling well. When he got home, the patio was set up for dinner for two. A four-course meal was served to them by a chef. Another time Dad left her a note to be ready at three o'clock in the afternoon. At three sharp he pulled into the driveway and picked her up. He wouldn't tell her where they were going. They drove into a large field with a hot air balloon, and they rode above the countryside. The stories went on and on.

The best one, I thought, was the way he asked her to marry him. He taped a red rose outside on the kitchen window. She went out to take off the rose, and there was a note saying, "Go to the car." She went to the car to find another rose and a note "Go to the yellow house with the green trim." It was a house that had not changed colors since 1921. She drove over, and, of course, there was another rose and note. This one said, "Go to our special church."

When she got to the church, she saw a whole bouquet of roses. There were thirty-six of them, thirty-five red, one white. The note read, "You are one of a kind. Will you marry me?" On the corner of the note it said, "over please." She turned it over and the message continued, "If you want to marry me come inside the church, and if you don't come inside, I will settle for a kiss."

"Dad, I didn't know you were such a romantic."

"I haven't told you even half of the stories. There were so many special moments. We both had to work at it, but I think we were the happiest couple in America."

"Look at this photograph, Dad."

It was Adam and I sitting on a donkey, on our way down into the basin of the Grand Canyon. That set off a whole new round of stories mostly about Adam and me. One of my favorites was when Adam and I thought we were drivers having learned to drive Dad's truck at twelve, and decided we also knew how to drive the tractor. We got it started without permission and promptly drove it into the ditch and broke the neighbor's fence. We didn't tell anyone, but three days later when the neighbor towed it out, we finally had to tell Dad. He wasn't too happy, but quickly got over it.

After so many stories, I was surprised at how quickly four o'clock came around. I didn't know how special Zach really was until this day. He was a romantic. A warm, creative, and generous man — he was my father.

"Dad, you are quite a character."

"Well, I was in my time, but you're not too bad yourself."

At that moment Pat pulled in with the truck. It was large, so we helped him back it into the driveway. We helped him load up all the boxes that were going into storage, and between the three of us, it went pretty fast. Afterwards he came in for some refreshments. Before he left he said he'd be back the next day at eight.

Boy, my dad was punctual. I looked at the clock — seven-thirty in the morning. Just time to dress and eat before Pat was to arrive.

"You better get moving. Pat's never late."

I just grumbled and pulled the sheet over my head. He's got to be kidding. This bed feels too good to leave. Five more minutes, that's all I needed.

"Alex, it's 7:50. Get up."

I must have dozed off again. Dad is standing over me, pulling the sheet. The sun was in my face. I guess there's no escape, so I smile at him and say, "Good morning, Dad. What's for breakfast?"

"Nothing if you don't get up right now."

"Be right there."

He walked out of the room. I jumped up and slipped into some clothes, brushed my teeth, combed my hair, and went into the kitchen. An orange juice was waiting and the toaster was working overtime. The whole morning was happening. Pat arrived, and Dad went to the door to let him in.

"Sit down and have some coffee," Dad greeted him.

He joined me at the table while I finished my breakfast, "How is everything, Pat?"

"Not bad. Ready to go to the big town?"

Trying to wake up, I slurred, "Think so."

We finished our food and got into the car and headed for the

Glimmer Of Hope shelter. Peggy was waiting for us. "Morning, Gentlemen. Rick is waiting for you. I'll tell him you are here."

Zach nodded his head. Almost immediately Rick came out of the shelter and walked up to us. "Gentlemen, we have to meet him at the Laughing Oyster downtown across from the library. He said he'd meet me at eleven." So off we went.

We got to the place just before eleven and sat down at a table. The place wasn't very busy, and we sit down at the back of the restaurant. A voice popped into my head out of the blue.

"Morning, Alex. You thought I had disappeared."

"Dad, could you sit somewhere else with Pat and Rick?"

He understood immediately and asked Pat and Rick to follow him. "What's going on, brother?" I asked.

"Listen, Alex. This is going to be tough, but follow your instincts, and let the flow of energy guide you. I will be right here in your heart and head." Adam had been gone for two or three days, and he'd come back unexpectedly.

"Where have you been, anyway?"

"Never mind. He's coming."

"How will he recognize me?"

"Just call him 'Nails' when he passes you."

A young man came in the restaurant. He looked around, walked pass Zach's table and continued without hesitation toward the back of the restaurant. Having not seen Rick, he turned and made eye contact with me which gave me the opportunity to address him, "Nails, sit down."

He looked at me surprised and with caution, suspicious of a clean guy knowing his name.

"I said, sit down," and showed him the chair. My voice had a commanding tone.

He just looked at me, sat down, and stared me in the eyes with disdain. "Tell me, Nails, what are you doing here?"

"I was supposed to meet Rick. I ain't talking to you. Just Rick."

"Relax. I'm here instead. Rick is over there at the other table."

"I don't know you. Get lost." He made a move as if he was going to get up and leave.

I looked at him. His eyes met mine, and he was literally thrown against the back of the chair. I had felt the energy go through my body.

"Let's talk," I said calmly, but with authority.

"Who are you?"

"Alex. Please to meet you, Nails. So tell me, why are you here?"

Still guarded, he answered, "I want out of the gang life."

"Any particular reasons?"

"I'm just tired, and I met a woman."

"Millions of people meet women," I pushed.

"She's pregnant, and I want my son to get more than a gang life."

"Why are you here?" I asked again.

"What's the matter with you? Are you deaf?" He squirmed in his chair still wanting to leave.

I looked him straight in the eyes, grabbed his hand and held it tight. Something was guiding me, it was beyond my control. I whispered, "The real reason, Nails."

"I'm scared," he admitted.

"Scared of your step-dad. Mad at the way he abused you and beat you, and so you decided to become a gang member to hide your fear. The thing you didn't count on was that the fear didn't go away, and now you're a slave to your reality. You're a slave to the fear, prisoner of the gang you founded, afraid to be called a coward."

Nails was looking at me like he was seeing me for the first time.

"Scared?" I pressed on. "We're all scared. There's no free ride in life. Maybe your step-dad was bad, maybe he did wrong, but who cares? Nobody cares, not even your step-dad. It happened long ago. He doesn't even remember it, but you allow him to control you by not forgiving and leading your own life."

"What do you want me to do?"

"I don't want you to do anything. If you want to do something for yourself, if you really want to get on with your life, first let go of your step-dad and the anger. Start fighting for yourself, no more hiding behind the tough guy image. Make your own decisions for a change."

"I make my own decisions," he insisted.

"You have never made a decision. You just imposed tough man rules, but you never feel good inside. You are a prisoner of your own rules, a decision is to take a stand and stick to it and never let go."

"How do I know if the decision is right?"

"When it feels good, it is right."

He sat calmly now without a word for several moments. Then he looked at me and asked, "Where do I start?"

"One, you stand proud of who you are. Two, stand up for your lady. She deserves a man, not someone who hides behind fear. Three, stand up for your son when he comes into this world. Give him the love you never got, give him everything you never had — security, discipline, education, friendship. Give him a father, for god's sake."

Nails had a hard time containing himself, "Maybe you're right."

"Just one rule. If you break it, we can't help you because support is the only thing we can give to you. It's all up to you"

"And the rule is?"

"You fight tooth and nail for a better life, and we'll help."

"Deal."

"See those people at that table? I will introduce you to them. They will never let you down. They'll always be in your corner. Don't let them down. Remember your little lady and your future son."

"I won't forget."

"By the way, what's your name? Your given name?"

"Ralph."

"Ralph, I won't tell, if you don't like it."

"Ralph it is. You just told me to stand proud." His back straightened as he spoke.

"All right, Ralph. Let me introduce you to everybody."

Just now I realized I was still holding his hand. They were sweaty. We went over to the table where the other guys were sitting, and I introduced him to everybody. Everyone said, "Hi Ralph," at once.

"Sit down with us," said Pat.

"Someone told me there would be two of you," said Rick.

"Don't worry. I will be bringing over as many of my friends as possible, including my lady friend."

The restaurant was almost full. Everyone was there for lunch. We ordered our food and chatted about different rules regarding the "Glimmer of Hope" shelter.

"I heard that all the homeless run the entire operation with only a little supervision," said Ralph.

"We try to give people responsibility and give them a chance to show us their talents and determination. By the way, we expected a lot more trouble," said Zach.

"I snuck out early this morning and walked around until it was time to meet you," confessed Ralph.

"That was a good idea."

"For me, I don't care, but it's for Isabelle. I don't want to stir up any trouble for her."

"Is that your young lady's name?" Zach inquired.

"Yeah, but in the street we call her 'Cheetah.' You'll see when you meet her." He was relaxing and actually smiling when he spoke.

Rick was experienced now and really adept at helping people develop their talents, so he wanted to get down to business, "Ralph, what can you do, or what would you like to do? We need to find you a responsible position."

"Not very much. I dropped out of school, but I can read and write. My spelling is pretty good. I can drive and I helped on a construction site, mainly digging and laying pipe. I also loaded and unloaded construction material."

"Would you like to become a bricklayer?" Rick questioned.

"I can give it a try."

"Good. Take a few days to get settled in at the shelter. We have a room for you and panther, or is it cheetah?" That made us all laugh. Zach was great at breaking the ice and making everyone feel at ease. "Let's make it Isabelle," Ralph recommended.

"Do you need help moving your stuff?"

"Not really. I ain't got much, nothing worth getting. I just need to get my lady."

"Good. The shelter is open twenty-four hours a day. At night we close the door, but if you ring the bell, someone will open it and let you in."

Ralph got up immediately after eating and thanked us for everything.

"You will have some problems with Nails," Adam said to me.

"Why is that?"

"All the other kids will see it as a betrayal. They will get angry, but don't worry, I will be watching over him."

"All right, Adam, but don't forget, I want to get my soul back."

"You sure are impatient, Brother.

"Never mind, bc careful out there."

Zach looked at me. He had heard the inner conversation. "Don't worry, Alex, your brother will take care of himself." Without thinking, he had spoken out loud.

Pat and Rick looked at him like he was nuts. "Zach, your son's been dead a long time."

"I know, Pat, but I still can think of him, can't I?"

"It just seems odd you bringing him up, never mind, I won't ask."

We took a load over to the Glimmer of Hope and visited with Peggy and the others. As for me, it was time to see Maggie. *I am getting pretty fond of my special friend*, I thought to myself.

There was a lot of activity going on. Gary was washing a car, two other kids were vacuuming out a car over near the building with another guy buffing a truck nearby. Theresa was sitting in a chair watching the little kids. Butterball stuck his head out of a black limo as he pulled up beside us. "Hey guys. Are you going to give us a hand?"

Zach and I just looked at him too surprised to answer. Another car was pulling into the lot and believe me, this was not a shabby heap. It was a late model with all the bells and whistles.

"Looks like you need an explanation," said Butterball as he came over and shook hands with everyone.

"It would help," said Zach with a smile.

Butterball turned to Rick. "Thanks for keeping the secret. Now, you tell them."

We all turned to look at Rick. "You have been so nice to us, so we wanted to show you we were capable and dedicated enough to start our own business."

I immediately understood where he was coming from. "You started your own detailing business," I said.

"Yeah. One Eye came up with the idea. We printed up some

flyers and saturated the business district downtown as well as industrial section. We pick up the cars before noon, clean them up, and bring them back before the business closes. It's going better than expected."

"How do you cope with insurance?"

"Twenty five percent of what we make goes into a special account for that purpose."

"And taxes?" I continued with the questions and became impressed with their thoroughness.

"That's your dad's department."

Dad spoke up. "What do you mean, my department?"

"Well, we send all the receipts to your accountant in a shoe box. We don't know how to do the paper work yet."

"I guess I will have to arrange it with my firm."

"We already did, Mister Zach."

"Who picks up the cars and delivers them?" I asked.

"We do. We're all dressed up, polite, and it's just great. Our first customer was the mayor. We gave him a discount, and he's recommended us to his staff and all of his friends."

"Keep coming up with good ideas." Zach said as he shook hands with Rick and Butterball.

M aggie was standing just behind me, and I didn't even notice until she put her hand on my shoulder prompting me to turn around.

"Hi, Alex. Glad you made it. I've missed you."

"I've missed you too, Maggie. I was hoping to see you."

I noticed that she had a duffle bag beside her as well as a large box. Pat was already grabbing the box and the duffle bag.

"What's in the box and bag?" I questioned.

Zach joined us, "Son, she is coming out to the house to spend a few days with us."

"I don't understand."

"She had asked me if there were any openings at the office, so she is going to ride into the office with me four days a week to work in the morning while she is being trained," he explained.

"So that is why you and Janice were straightening up the house."

Dad actually blushed and gave me one of his don't say anything else glares, "Never mind Alex."

"And I wondered who you were redecorating the guest room for. Guess I'll have to be a good boy and help around the house. All kidding aside, I'm glad you're coming for a visit." I grabbed her hand as I spoke.

She remained speechless during the whole conversation and just gave me a hug, when I made it clear I was just as happy as she was about the plan.

"Now let's go inside and see how Peggy is doing." Zach, Maggie and I walked in leaving the rest of the group working on the cars. Each proudly doing their job and building self-respect in the process.

Maggie pointed out the new plants that she and Mary had added to the hallway and the dining room to make it more homey and informal. There was a dark, four-foot fig tree, a couple of hibiscus plants and at least six or eight large ferns hanging from the ceiling. I noticed all the original pictures on the wall and asked, "Where did all the artwork come from?"

"Theresa has started a contest for all age groups, and we display their work here," Maggie explained.

"How does it work?"

"There are different categories not only age groups but also for subject matter, design and medium. Mostly it's just a way to reward their creative efforts."

"So what is the grand prize?" my curious nature showing itself.

"It depends on the category. Why do you want to know so much about it?"

"I don't know, maybe, I want to enter," I teased.

"Kinda depends on the age group. There are movie tickets, rollerblade passes for the arena, new t-shirts, cassettes and video games, coupons for free hamburgers, and we are still collecting donations."

"How do you get donations?"

"We just explain to the merchants what we are trying to do for the kids and young people, and ask them to help us out. After all they gain also from getting the kids off the streets — less shoplifting and petty theft, so most of them give graciously," Maggie explained putting her hand in mine again.

"Alex, why are you asking so many questions?" Dad interrupted.

"I'm excited, and I'm looking for how I can participate."

"Good, then participate, but don't talk her ear off."

"It's okay, Mr. Beard, I know how curious he can be."

"Listen, Maggie, it's Zach and not Mr. Beard, and he's my son, but he has to learn to be patient."

Peggy saw us in the dining room and walked in our direction her hand in her white apron, her hair pulled back except for a few wisps hanging down around her face, smiling as usual. "Good day, Zach."

"Peggy, you look ravishing."

"You charming devil. I know it's not true since I've worked all morning, but any compliment is wonderful to hear."

"I've got many more, Peggy, you inspire me."

"Dad, stop you're going to make her blush."

"Make *me* blush, Alex, I'm too old to blush." She laughed as she came over and took me in her arms. Her gentleness had the magic to let you know that you were loved. "I heard that Maggie is going to stay at your house."

"Yes, in fact I just found out," my pleasure showing in my face as I spoke.

"You treat her right or you'll have to answer to me. Now go on with Maggie. I need to talk to your dad."

We walked out back to watch the detailing car operation, they were down to the last three cars with someone just pulling the next car around. We held hands while waiting for Dad. One of the teens started a sponge fight, and we decided to back off before we got soaked. Dad and Peggy came out of the building still talking.

"Alex, can I talk to you a moment?" a voice beckoned me from behind. I turned to the left and Rick was standing behind me frowning. I excused myself from Maggie and walked over to join him. "What's going on?"

"It's Bill. He is starting to act strangely again, and I spotted Simon snooping around."

"I will talk to my dad, and within the next ten days we will do something about it."

"I appreciate your concern," Rich seem relieved.

"Glad you brought it to my attention, and I'll also talk to Bill."

"He's right over there." Rick motioned toward the building.

"I guess right now is about as good a time as any. Hey Bill, Bill, got a minute?" I shouted over the screams of happiness from the water fight that had gotten out of hand.

He finally heard me and walked over to where we were standing after tripping over the garden hose, losing his balance and almost landing in my face. "Bill, what's going on with Simon?"

"The turkey found me. I don't want to hide all my life, and ever since I saw him the nightmares have increased."

"Hang in there. I am working on it with Dad's help," seeing his fear I wanted to let him know that there was hope.

"In the meantime I'll just stay around the shelter."

He looked scared, not as bad as when we found him over a year ago, but still very shaken. I reassured him as Zach was saying goodbye to Peggy.

We got into the car, and Dad and I talked telepathically about Bill's fear and the harassment from Simon deciding to talk about it more intensively at the house. Pat and Maggie had been chatting in the backseat so we joined in and enjoyed the scenery for the rest of the trip home. Maggie noticed the big white house with the grey roof, gingerbread trim and the three story turret on the side.

"I have never seen anything like this. Alex, look at least twenty columns on the side of the house with two round gazebos attached to the house, a balcony over the front porch, and a double carport on the back. I wonder who lives there," she commented.

We turned left, then went over the railroad tracks and drove by the yellow house with green trim. The colors of the house hadn't changed since 1921, and now it was a classy grill eatery. Maggie is charmed by the picturesque aspects of the small town.

"I am going to like it here," she declared.

"We hope you do," said Zach. "There is not much night life."

"I worked six nights a week for almost four years, so I could use a little rest at night, it will be nice spending my days looking at the trees, the flowers, the blue sky and listening to the birds for a change."

"You will certainly find a slower pace in this town, my dear."

Once we pulled into the driveway Pat grabbed one bag, and I

picked up the box. Zach led Maggie into the house and showed her the way to the guest bedroom, which had been specially prepared for her with new curtains and towels in the adjoining bath. He gave her instructions on how to adjust the window air conditioner to her comfort and told her to make herself at home.

Leaving her to get settled he joined us in the living room placing his feet up. "I am bushed. It won't be long before I am ready to retire," Dad yawned.

Pat got up, "I'm pretty beat myself so if you will excuse me, I'll be on my way." He walked out the door after shaking our hands.

Zach went out to the back porch for a breath of fresh air while I turned on the television and watched the news. They were talking about a big industrial leader making a multimillion dollar deal with the government revamping the computer system for the employee payroll.

"That's the man, the one with the black hair on the left side of the chief of staff to the white house." I will never get use to Adam popping in and out of my head talking without warning. "Hi, Alex, did I scare you again?"

"Never mind, what did you say about the man with the black hair?" I asked.

"That man right here," he pointed with my arm at the television. Without effort Adam was controlling it. "You see this man, right there, his soul was one of the ones we retrieved from Lazlo. I reunited his spirit with his body."

"But he's a big wig."

"You bet, and they were blackmailing him for information,"

Adam reminded me.

"What is Lazlo's organization trying to do?"

"Lazlo was just one of the members of the organization. We must find the power behind all this mess."

"How can we do that?"

"I don't know but I am working on it, and Clay's got some ideas."

"You find out all you can, and Dad and I will be ready to help."

Maggie walked into the room, so I said goodbye to Adam. She sat down beside me and watched a little television while holding hands. Dad came back from the porch looked in the door to say good night and left for his room. She fell asleep in my arms while watching a program. I slipped my arm from under her head and got up to go to the refrigerator to get a glass of juice.

"Will you bring me back something to drink?" she lazily requested.

"Coming up." I brought the glasses of juice back to the living room. She was stretching as I joined her on the couch. We flicked the channels for a few minutes and found nothing to our liking so we turned it off and talked awhile.

Not realizing how tired we were, we both fell asleep and woke up about two AM having not even touched our juices. Standing up and stretching I realized how sore my muscles were and after a gentle good night kiss, we wandered to our individual rooms.

The next few days were absolutely charming. We took long walks all over the town, strolled around the lake holding hands. We even went out to a nearby farm early one morning to pick blueberries for breakfast. I was making the most of our time knowing that she had to start to work at the office the next week. We went for ice cream, sat on the back porch while she supervised my attempt to barbecue on the grill, shopped for groceries and just soaked up the sun enjoying the lack of demands and our carefree moments.

I had asked about her family on one of our walks and listened as Maggie told me about growing up. She was an only child and things were really tough, especially after her dad just left when she was only thirteen. Her mom worked two, and sometimes three, jobs to pay the bills, but when Maggie was barely sixteen all the hard work caught up with her mom. Maggie dropped out of high school and got a job at a fast food chain. Less than a year later her mom died. The doctors said that it was cancer, but Maggie always suspected that she really died of a broken heart.

That was over three years ago. She had lived with a friend of her mom's for a year until she was able to get her GED by going to night school.

There was no anger or "poor me" in her voice. She had been at the coffee shop for over two years and actually liked it. Guess people felt it because with her tips she had gotten her own apartment and used car. Quite an accomplishment for a twenty year old.

Now she was excited about her new job and was planning to go back to night school to get a degree in accounting. The more that I learned about her the more I loved her.

I had never felt so relaxed and happy. There had been times as carefree a long time ago when my brother and I were together, but this was now.

Toward the end of the week, Maggie wondered out loud, "Why have you never talked about your childhood, your dad, and the wonderful town you grew up in?"

"I had some memory problems, but I would rather not talk about it." I realized that our relationship was deepening, and I couldn't avoid the whole truth much longer. But perhaps I would have my spirit back before I had to worry her.

"Was this related to the nightmares?"

"Exactly," I answered, just hoping that she would be patient a little longer.

"Well I am glad everything is all right, and we can forget about the past."

"Not really. I still have some work ahead of me." *That's an understatement*, I thought to myself.

"May I ask."

If she pushed, I was prepared to be honest, I did love her, but please, please don't let her push for details. "No, just trust me."

"Pork chops are ready. Would you mind getting our drinks while I serve and put the sour cream on the potatoes."

"Will do." I went into the kitchen to get more ice relieved that she had changed the subject so quickly. I didn't really want to explain until this ordeal was completely over. I returned with the glasses in my hand. She had brought our plates out to the table, the food still steaming.

As we sat down we were entertained by two squirrels defying

the laws of gravity jumping back and forth from the branch overhanging the porch to the roof to the guardrail back up the tree. I sat down, and she passed me the dressing for the salad. Eating in silence I could tell that she was a little miffed at my not telling her, but what could I say not knowing how everything would turn out. Will I get my soul back, and how could I explain that I still communicated with my dead brother? Talk about a perfect recipe to test a friendship, I decided to keep it to myself for the time being.

"Come on, Maggie, smile at me. The food is great, but I need the cook to smile at me to make me appreciate the flavor of it."

She gave me a faint smile.

"You can do better than that. You're left side is still not smiling and that is your best side," I teased.

She pulled my head over to her and gave me a kiss on the cheek. "You better tell me all the details when it is over."

"I promise, but for now you must smile."

The rest of the evening was spent listening to music and talking. Zach came in late and joined us. He had eaten earlier so he just sat down to share his day.

"Signed a contract to help build the new arena attached to the conference center that I helped build two years ago. You know, in the north part of town."

I could sense his pride. "Sounds like a pretty good day," I remarked.

"I would say so. I even purchased the adjoining building to the Glimmer of Hope."

"What for?" I asked, realizing immediately the answer seeing him as the magnanimous man who was also my father.

"Well, it dawned on me that there are only five rooms left with Ralph moving in with Isabelle, and with so many more kids on the street, we are going to need more space shortly."

"Zach, you are such a super guy," Maggie exclaimed as she jumped out of her chair to hug his neck. Good thing I'm not the jealous type.

"Enough of that you two or I'll have to get another girlfriend," I teased. So they just laughed and hugged some more before she came back over to the couch and sat down.

Dad proceeded to tell her some embarrassing anecdotes about my childhood. He told them so well that he had both of us in tears from laughing so hard.

Around eleven o'clock we all cleaned up the kitchen leaving the crumbs for the squirrels for their morning snack.

"Alex, it is time to get ready for action." It was late in the afternoon. Maggie and I had shared one of our perfect days, and I had just gone up to my room to shower and rest a little before dinner.

"Where have you been, Adam?"

"Gathering information and all my strength. We are going to need it tonight."

"You mean we go after my soul tonight?" My entire being responded with anticipation.

"Yeah, no turning back now. Dad and you are driving into town tonight."

"I can't wait."

"Well, I don't know how it will turn out."

"Swell, we are driving in the dark. So why tonight, what makes it so special?"

"Simon's been entertaining, and he told his maid that he was going to stay in tonight and gave her the night off." He had been doing his homework.

"It sounds like you've been spying on Simon."

"Of course, you want your soul back or not?"

"You know I do."

"Well, then get ready. We are leaving soon." His impatience showing itself as usual.

"Should I tell Dad?" as I slipped on my jeans, knowing the

answer before I asked it, but heard, "He knows."

Zach knocked at my door at that precise moment to tell me to get ready. I startled him when I opened the door so quickly with my shirt in my hand.

"I see that Adam came in to pay you a visit," he observed.

"Yes, so when are we leaving?" My excitement had kicked in.

"As soon as you tell Maggie."

"Where is she?"

"Reading a book in the living room."

I went to the living room, and no one was there. Turning to leave I saw her sitting in the study in the recliner, the light from the lamp shining softly on her face and book. I tenderly observed her through the open door for a few seconds, "Maggie, sorry to interrupt you, but Dad and I are leaving."

"Will you be late?" she asked as she closed her book and stretched her arms over her head.

"Don't know, but don't wait up for us."

"Have a good night." She blew me a kiss and went back to her book. I spent a few more seconds admiring her before pivoting on my heel and joining Zach in the car. He backed out of the driveway, and we were on the road rolling in the direction of the big city.

"Do you have any plans, Dad?"

He was negotiating a rather sharp curve, "Not really, but with Adam and Clay's help, I think we can handle it."

"So Clay is coming with us." I was watching the terrain change as we approached the four lane, trying to keep my mind occupied.

"Yes, I phoned about fifteen minutes ago and believe me, we will need all of his expertise to pull enough energy if we want to be successful."

"What do you mean, if we want to be successful? We've got to be successful, I want back what is mine. I can't believe we're talking about this so nonchalantly."

"Relax, we will all do our best, Son."

"I sure hope so." I realized my reply was a little sharp. I guess I am a little more tense than I realized. I've waited so long for this moment, and we are so close...

"Do you think that the snake is still alive?" Snakes have a long life expectancy was an ample answer for my silly question. "Man, that thing was large, bigger around than my waist and seemed like twenty feet long." I shivered just remembering. "I must say that Simon has a sense of humor — he called it Slider."

Adam jumped in, "Don't underestimate him, you two. You will need all of your mental capacity, so you two better pay attention and concentrate when you are in his presence."

"So what do you want us to do?" asked Zach.

After all, Adam did have the most knowledge in these matters, and if we wanted to be successful, we had to trust and follow his lead. His answer kinda surprised us.

"I know that it seems crazy, but we are going to have to play it by ear. I mean that we going to have to improvise again."

"Great, Adam, I don't think that the snake trick will work a second time so I guess we had better be ready to tap dance." My stress level accelerated.

"Don't be so negative, Alex, I know you're anxious about your soul, but we're all here so give us a chance. We've got to stay calm, work together, and have faith." Adam made sense.

I still felt like we needed a plan, "So we just walk up to the door and ring the bell and scream 'Trick or treat'?"

"That's enough, Alex," reprimanded Zach, "but on second thought, it just might work."

"You mean go to the front door and ring the bell. It is a rather bold approach," Adam mused.

"Why not?" Zach cradled his chin between his thumb and index finger, rubbed his chin and continued, "The element of surprise just might work."

When he sees the three of us, he will lock the door and barricade himself inside, I thought.

"Oh no, you forget how pretentious he is and when you got arrogant, he lost his cool. Don't you remember my dear brother?" Alex reminded me

"You have a point."

"Well, nobody in their right mind would knock on their worst enemy's door with a smile on their face." Zach offered.

"Listen, Adam, I think you're crazy," I said, "But you know, it just might work. The last time I saw Simon, he had one hell of an attitude."

We arrived at the intersection right by the old fire station that had been transformed into a clothing store. Clay had arrived and was waiting for us.

Zach opened his window while pulling the last few yards in Clay's direction. Clay greeted us as we stepped out of the car to plan our strategy, discussing a few options, but the gutsy approach of ringing the doorbell seemed the most logical.

All of us got into Dad's car and continued the journey to Simon's house. By now the tension was mounting. I asked if I'm the only one who's nervous.

"No, the anxiety is causing knots in my stomach," Clay admitted.

"Me, too, Son, if we weren't nervous I'd think something was wrong with all of us."

"You bunch of chickens," Adam taunted, hovering above us.

"Be quiet, you shadow," I replied, "all you have to do is fly away or go up the chimney like Santa."

"You made your point, Brother, but I won't let you down. Just trying to loosen you guys up a little."

A couple of turns on the winding country road and the driveway to the mansion turned off to the right sharply. We slowed down, and the car rolled into the driveway by the front door. The silence is deafening, almost painful. We've got to relax a little I think to myself with Adam agreeing as we stepped out of the car.

There was a light visible through the sheer curtains on the front of the house. I don't know about the others, but I had cold sweat running down my back. The light cast an eery shadow over the holly bushes along the front porch. The silence weighed heavier as we approach the door.

Who's going to ring the bell? I thought to myself. That's something we should have discussed before we all got here. Too late now.

An almost imperceptible squeak came from the door which was open and still moving, we all focused on the front door. Our eyes riveted to the ray of light enlarging as the door swung on its hinges. Simon appeared in the doorway looking at us and shaking his head.

"Good evening, you clowns. Oh, don't tell me let me guess, you must be here to reclaim Alex's soul. Well, well, well. Come on inside. As you can see I am not threatened by you, although I might observe that doesn't appear to apply to the bunch of you trembling in your shoes."

The energy around him was incredible. We could feel the evil in his voice. He was confident to the point of arrogance.

"What are you waiting for? Enter. I have felt your vibrations for some time now. All of you together don't have enough power to overcome me."

The guy is going to trip on his ego. I felt a powerful blow across my head and found myself flat on my face lying in the center of the driveway.

"I heard that you little punk," Simon addressed me.

"Touchy, touchy, man get a life," I replied.

Simon looked at me and made me slide with great force against the bushes. "I will deal with you later." He turned and entered the house.

Somehow Zach and Clay were mesmerized, following Simon in the house like they had been drugged. They disappeared from my vision, and I tried to regain my composure after having the wind knocked out of me. Getting up was a chore, but I forced myself to a standing position, walked up to the four steps to the porch, opened the front door and stepped into the hallway.

Dad and Clay were in the living room at the far end of the room, a lady was seated on the sofa. She is gracious in her gestures and her look was stunning. The snake curled up on the recliner taking the whole chair has seemingly increased in size since our last encounter several months ago. Simon stood facing them with his back to me unaware or uninterested in my presence.

"What is happening?" questioned the charming lady.

"Quiet," said Simon, "this won't take long."

He turned his attention to Clay and Dad and laughed at them, "So you are trying to reclaim what you think is yours."

"Yes, I have come to deliver the souls you are wrongfully holding." Clay answered.

A pristine serenity came into my heart, and suddenly I realized my power to harness the energy of the universe. We are so aware of our physical body, and totally ignore the power of our spirit. I acknowledged this truth and felt an unearthly peace as I anchored myself, gathering strength little by little with no limits in my mind. Adam became conscious of my feelings and what I was attempting. He joined in my efforts pulling from the limitless supply of energy around us. Simon's attention was focused on Clay as he prepared to eliminate him as a threat.

"Simon, why do you viciously terrorize people anyway?" I

asked very convincingly.

"So you've joined us," he continued, "because when I extract other people's spirit it not only keeps me young, but it gives me power, supreme power, and I can control anyone I want."

"Big deal. So you use other people's spirit because you are too weak to make it on your own." If anybody had ever gotten him angry, I just hit the jackpot for enraging him. His face turned red, his fists tighten to the point of turning his knuckles white, his whole body was trembling out of control.

"Temper, temper, temper. There is a lady present," I said in hopes of aggravating him more.

Simon stayed in control, "You have no soul and are, therefore, insignificant to me."

"Maybe, but you are still an incomplete man without the spirits of others."

I don't know why but I felt that his anger would make him lose his grip over the powers he controlled, so I continued to nag him. His face was as red as a beet.

The lady was getting impatient, "I would really like to know what is going on?"

Simon addressed her without taking his eyes off me, "Claire, I told you to be quiet and not interfere."

"I am surprised at your total lack of manners," I taunted him.

"I have a special punishment in mind for you later, but for now I must take care of your friends," he said as he turned around ignoring me completely which is just what I have been waiting for.

I took a deep breath and pulled the energy from him. I pulled with all of my mental strength calling upon the universe to help me. I didn't let go, I felt energy coming from the four corners of the universe. Adam joined in, and we were now pulling together. For a split second Simon stood very still, and then an inhuman scream emerged from his lungs.

While turning on his heels the scream intensified as his face became hideously deformed. Adam and I intensified our efforts, and the miracle happened — like a blooming flower one soul emerged from his body. Simon's face was changing, the excruciating pain tore his body apart, his face had aged before my eyes by at least fifty years.

He tried to regain control, but Clay and Zach had joined their forces to pull from him, and he convulsed as three other souls emerged from the form that had once been Simon's body as it shriveled under the convulsions starting to dematerialize as we watched. We slowly let go of the energy when all that was left was a pile of dust.

The lady was petrified. Clay went quickly over to the open china cabinet, grabbed a bottle of sherry and a glass to take to the lady and poured her a glass. "Drink," he directed.

She did not move terrified by the developments. Her acquaintance had just been dematerialized, she had the right to be hysterical to say the least. Clay spoke softly to her while she slowly returned to the reality that we were not there to harm her. She sipped the sherry and a little blush returned to her cheeks.

Zach said the first words, "You can control a soul, but you can not own it. So be it."

"Amen," we replied. For once we all agreed in unison.

In all of the chaos the snake has not moved one inch, he must have been fed in the last week, so much for its loyalty to his owner. He even looked content curled up in his chair.

Clay is back to business. "Now let's take care of the souls."

"I forgot about it in the heat of the moment. Where is mine anyway?" As I spoke I felt Adam's presence leaving my body. It was a strange sensation, tingling in every cell, every pore, from the follicles in my toenails to the shafts of my hair. Everything leaving my body all the feelings — passion, peace, love, hope, tenderness, forgiveness, and joy just as it had entered. The sensations were all leaving at once, like the roots of a tree being pulled out of the earth. I felt a shiver down my back.

One of the souls detached itself from the other three and moved toward my physical body, it hesitated for an instant, wrapped itself around me and started to seep inside of me. The process had been reversed and everything that I had felt leaving was now being restored, but this time it was all my own feelings and sensations. The void had been filled, but I felt strange.

"Alex," I asked myself, "are you here?"

"No, you're not entirely," Adam answered.

"What do you mean?" My anxiety was mounting. *Maybe my soul got used up*, I thought.

Hearing my fears, Adam comforted me, "Well, your soul has been trapped for over four years. Now it will need some rest, so it has stored itself inside of you, and slowly it will start feeling your essence, remembering everything, and you will merge or blend."

"How long will that process of blending take?" I felt a twinge of joy in my heart as his words sunk in.

"Two or three weeks depending on how damaged your spirit has been, so let it rest."

"How do I do that?"

"Stay calm and don't get emotional."

"Whatever you say. I'll give it my best. You know I will." I suddenly realized that I hadn't expressed my gratitude for Adam's help. Before I could voice it, he said, "What are brothers for, and now I've got work to do." He swirled and joined the three other souls.

He came back quickly to Dad and Clay. I could hear him loud and clear. He was going to be able to bring one of the souls back to its body. It was very tired, and its spirit had been almost dissipated. The other two were unrestorable, one was Jack's. While Adam was talking Jack's spirit came to me.

I could barely see the form, but as it faded it whispered to me, "Take care of yourself." Now he could complete his destiny and pass on.

Adam escorted Bill's soul to reunite it with his body.

"Adam, tell Bill that I will see him at Glimmer of Hope as soon as possible." I really couldn't wait to see, feel, and be myself and share it all with Bill. He would be the only one who could share the joy of experiencing the miracle.

Clay got up to refill the lady's glass and told Adam to give Bill his regards.

Dad was sitting with the lady comforting her explaining our

actions. I felt strange with my soul inside me, but not capable of communicating my feelings.

"Sorry to interrupt, Zach, but I remember a small detail from my previous visit here."

"What is it, Son?"

"Simon mentioned that he had a box with papers that allowed him to change his identity at will."

"What papers are you talking about?"

"I don't recall exactly. The last time I saw him I was angry and wasn't thinking straight, and I ended up in a coma, but I know that it seemed important."

Dad got up and took me by the arm leading me over to Clay after excusing himself from Claire. He explained to Clay my recollection of some papers.

"Alex, do you have any idea where that box could be?"

"Not really, but he did say they were within hand's reach."

Dad and Clay decided that the best course of action was to search the house. After all, there might be clues to others in the organization or the identity of souls who were under the control of the organization or who were their targets in the future.

"What are we waiting for?" Clay said with excitement.

We concentrated our search in the study. The massive desk was probably too obvious, but seemed like a good place to start. There in the second drawer on the left was a metal box. Opening it up we found a stack of birth certificates, social security cards, and a deed to some property. Zach picked up the deed, "This deed has never been assigned to anyone."

"What does that mean, Dad?"

"Well, Son, it means that this house can be deeded to anyone whose name we place on this deed."

Clay found some other notes and files that didn't make any sense. He picked up all the papers and notes and put them in a large folder. "I'll go through these later, but I think it is time to get out of here."

"What about the lady?" We all turned around at Zach's words. She was sitting motionless looking at the sherry glass in her hand.

"We'll take her with us."

"And the snake?" I asked as if I cared, but it could give someone a heart attack or there was no telling what it would do if it got hungry.

"We can call the zoo in the morning," Dad quickly answered.

"Great idea," we all concurred.

"Actually I was kidding, but you are right, we might as well make a donation to the zoo."

Zach stepped into the living room to offer to take Claire back into the city. She was still in a daze but seemed relieved and gratefully accepted. Clay and I walked out to the car and waited for them. Zach helped Claire into the car, and we drove in silence to Clay's car. He smiled as he got into his car.

"Good job you guys, but I fear that there is much work to be done ahead. I'll call you in a few days after I've looked over the papers."

"Thank you, Clay," was all Dad and I could say at the moment.

We drove to the shelter, Dad and I exhausted and relieved, Claire still visibly shaken by the events of the preceding few hours. I could feel Dad directing his healing energy toward her, and I couldn't help but wonder who she was and what she was doing there.

Although it was quite late when we arrived, the shelter was alive with activity with Bill standing outside. He could hardly contain himself when we drove up. We hadn't even come to a full stop when he grabbed the car door trying to open it thanking me profusely. "Alex, I've got it, I felt it, I've got it back. The fear is gone."

"Calm down," I said still sitting in the car.

"Why calm down? I feel too good."

As I got out of the car I put my arms around Bill, "Yes, Bill, but your soul needs rest, so chill a little. I'm telling you to just relax for the next few weeks."

"If you say so, but it's going to be hard."

He went around introducing himself to everyone as if he had just arrived on the scene himself.

We walked into the dining room where Peggy was talking to a young lady with stunning blue eyes and brown hair to her shoulders. She had a soft voice, but the hard look of the streets.

Peggy got up to greet us and led us to another table, "I will be right back with you." She went back over to the young lady and whispered a few words and called me over with a gesture. I excused myself and approached the table.

"Alex, have a seat. I want you to meet Isabelle. She's Ralph's friend."

"Pleased to meet you, Isabelle."

"How did you trick Ralph into coming here?" she asked with anger.

"You can go," I snapped as I showed her the door. "Grab your stuff. You are free to go."

"I think I'll just do that," as she reached for her bag.

By the time I stood up and turned to walk back to Zach and Claire she called, "Come back, Mister."

I turned around and saw a woman who had obviously been toughened by the street with a tired and forlorn look in her eyes, both arms hanging loosely by her sides, "I have nowhere to go."

"Let's start again," I replied and extended my hand, "my name is Alex. Welcome to Glimmer of Hope. This is your new home. Feel free to come and go as you please."

Isabelle apologized for being so rude while shaking my hand.

"No need to apologize. I was a street kid myself, and I know how hard it is to trust a stranger."

She relaxed a little so we sat down again and got to know each other a little better. She told me that she had been in the streets for four years. "I don't remember what it feels like to have a safe place to rest, clean sheets and a place to bathe."

"Don't worry because here you will be safe. You will have your own room, and there is always someone here to answer questions and help you. When is your child due?"

"In a couple of months, I think. I came here because I want my child to have a better life. There's no hope on the street."

I looked around the room and realized a truth as I spoke, "That's what this place is all about, Isabelle. Hope. Hope for all of us and your unborn child. By the way, I haven't seen Ralph."

"He'll be here in a couple of days. He is trying to convince Bumper to come here."

"Any particular reason why he needs convincing?" Each person who came here needed to be committed and responsible. We didn't force anyone.

"Because he is just scared like the rest of us."

"I understand." I had all of my memories back and, yes, I could remember and understand.

Zach got up and joined us at the table, "Everything okay?"

"Yes, Zach, just getting acquainted with Isabelle."

"So how do you like it here so far?" Dad asked.

"I don't know yet. It's all too new and seems to be too good to be true," she answered.

"You'll have plenty of time. Nobody will force you to do anything. When you are ready you will find a way to help others like yourself." Dad had an amazing ability of giving people hope and a sense of responsibility.

I sat there watching them with a lump in my throat. I was looking at hope, true hope.

My mind jumped to the picture of Maggie reading her book and could feel that now I had a future — we had a future.

Isabelle was shaking her head, "I guess I have never experienced the honesty and kindness that you are extending. It still puzzles me." Her eyes filled with tears and spilled over as Zach moved over to comfort her by tenderly holding her hand.

Hope is the dream of an awakened man...

To be continued . . .

ABOUT THE SEQUEL
(To be released early 1999)

Who was the woman at Simon's house in the last chapter and why was she there? Find out in the sequel as she becomes a major force and influence in the lives of Alex and Zach. Her knowledge and powers are instrumental in Alex's development of power and ability to erase the negative forces in the universe.

Alex travels in search of answers and is assisted by entities from a parallel dimension in time who pass to him the wisdom from ancient tribes. His encounters with the positive energies represented by loving, supportive, non-judgemental humans in this physical dimension, united with the support of the ancients, contribute to his emerging power. This power becomes a threat to those whose survival is based on exploitation and who are committed to destroying him. The adventures and characters contribute to the entertainment of the reader and also stimulate the imagination to see past the obvious.

The sequel continues the message that there is hope, and we must claim the power of positive thinking.

ABOUT THE AUTHOR

François Sigrist was born in Geneva, Switzerland, in 1949. Trained as a master chef in Europe, his profession over a twenty-five year career led him to positions in France, Germany, England, Canada, Central and South Americas, and the United States. He is fluent in five languages. For the last several years he has traveled extensively and devoted his time to documenting his impressions of people, places, and human behavior.

His first fictional novel reflects his observations and contacts with people all over the world, some whose spirits had been "stolen" by abuse, poverty, fear, and anger. He formulated and experienced the solutions through inspiring, supportive individuals who through love, forgiveness, acceptance, and communication were making a difference.

PUBLICATION SERVICES, INC.
8803 TARA LANE
AUSTIN, TEXAS 78737
(800)487-6093
Fax: (512) 288-5055
E-mail: orders@pubservices.com
http://www.pubservices.com

Retail Price: $19.95 (S & H $4.25)
Only $1.50 each (S & H) for 2nd, 3rd, & 4th copies.

****

FOR INFORMATION & INQUIRIES

WRITE TO:

AVERETTE PUBLICATIONS, INC.
P O BOX 685069
AUSTIN, TEXAS 78768

Treasure Hunt Results
Available by Written Request
After March 20, 1999 and
before April 20, 1999.

Shipping included on orders of twenty (20) or more.

GLIMMER OF HOPE
by François Sigrist

In times of seemingly monumental social problems too vast for anyone to address, the novel *GLIMMER OF HOPE* brilliantly brings to life characters who not only cope, but implement real solutions.

Meet characters who are symbolic — faceless, raceless, and homeless — caught in a void created when spirit is removed by a seemingly heartless society. Together they combine their energies and talents to regain their self-determination and self-respect, and awaken their community to their plight. Their youthful resourcefulness and value to the community is recognized when they are given a GLIMMER OF HOPE by just one entity.

Feel the essence of Alex, a naive youth, who is thrust into the streets through no fault or understanding on his part. The loss of his mother at birth and his twin at fifteen could easily explain his symptoms of despair, anger, depression, and fear. But imagine, if you will, a less obvious force, a subtle negative force capable at will of imposing these exact same emotional manifestations. Befriended by the likes of Lips, Butterball, and One Eye after having been stripped of his soul by this power, Alex attempts the journey to recover his spirit.

Tenaciously Alex unravels the mystery of his situation, and as the plot unfolds, finds support and solutions from young and old, new and familiar, real and spiritual entities. This classic, heroic tale simply emphasizes the power of hope, love, friendship, and survival.

The philosophy, with its directness of style and content and its message against drugs, hate, and fear, is not only suitable for an ageless audience, but it is also truly inspirational to all that there is a *GLIMMER OF HOPE*.

$500,000 IN CASH AND PRIZES

OFFICIAL RULES FOR TREASURE HUNT

No purchase necessary. Where prize entry instructions are included, entries that do not comply with all such instructions found elsewhere in this offer are not eligible. Sweepstakes begins 11/10/97. Entries must be received by 12/31/98. Residents of the United States are eligible to receive prizes. Prizes to be awarded: One (1) $250,000 First Prize; One (1) $100,000 Second Prize; One (1) $50,000 Third Prize; Fifty (50) $1,000 Fourth Prizes; 2,500 Runners-Up to receive book (valued at $20) which is the sequel to Glimmer Of Hope. Employees and immediate families of the author and Averette Publishing, Inc., its presenters, subsidiaries, distributors, advertising and promotional agencies are not eligible. Entries must include the name of the city, state, and zip code of the hometown of the main character in the book Glimmer Of Hope. Clues are available in the text of the book. Major winners may also be required to correctly answer a verbal question based on the contents of the book. Subject to all applicable laws and regulations. Void wherever prohibited or restricted.

Winners will be selected in a random drawing from all correct entries within sixty (60) days of the 12/31/98 deadline. Odds of winning depend upon the number of qualified entries received. Major winners will be notified via regular mail within fourteen (14) days of drawing. Only one (1) winner per household. Any prize notification returned as undeliverable results in awarding of that prize to an alternate at random. Prize winners must execute and return affidavit of eligibility and liability/ publicity release within fourteen (14) days of notification of award, or prize will be awarded to an alternate. Prizes won by minors must be awarded in the name of a parent or guardian who must execute affidavit and release on the minor's behalf. Prizes are not transferrable except to a surviving spouse. Entries from a third party or entries sent in bulk will not be accepted. Prizes to be awarded and will be delivered approximately sixty (60) days after receipt of affidavits. By entering, participants agree to these rules and expressly consent to the use of their name, photograph, or likeness for advertising or promoting this and similar promotions without compensation.

The following applies to all entries: to enter without an official entry form or purchase, print your name and address along with your solution to the Treasure Hunt on a postcard and mail to Averette Publications, Inc., P O Box 685069, Austin, Texas 78768. Upon receipt of a correct entry you will automatically qualify for all prizes offered herein should all other requirements be met. No photocopied or mechanically reproduced entries accepted. Entry materials that have been tampered with or altered are void. Sponsor not responsible for lost, late, misdirected, damaged, incomplete, illegible, or postage-due entries. All entries become sponsor's property and will not be returned. Any prize notice resulting from error will be void. All taxes (and any expenses not specified herein) including, but not limited to, income taxes are winner's responsibility.

For a list of winners, send a self-addressed, stamped envelope after 03/20/99 and before 04/20/99 to Averette Publications, Inc., P O Box 685069, Austin, Texas 78768.